GENEROSITY

UNDERSTANDING THE RICHES OF LIBERALITY

S. SEKOU ABODUNRIN

CW01666701

Generosity

Understanding the riches of liberality

Sekou Publishing

sekou@sekou.me

Copyright © 2018 by Sekou Abodunrin

Cover Design and Page Layout
Kenteba Kreations
contact.kenteba@gmail.com

ISBN: 978-1-912921-00-3

Published by Sekou Publishing. All rights reserved.

No part of this book may be reproduced in any form, by photocopying or by any electronic or mechanical means, including information storage or retrieval systems, without permission in writing from both the copyright owner and publisher of this book.

Unless otherwise indicated, all Scripture quotations are taken from the King James Version of the bible.

Some Scripture quotations marked (TPT) are taken from The Passion Translation (TPT) The Passion Translation®. Copyright © 2017 by BroadStreet Publishing® Group, LLC. Used by permission. All rights reserved. Thepassiontranslation.com

Some Scripture quotations marked "The Amplified" or (AMP) are taken from the Amplified® Bible, Copyright © 1954, 1958, 1962, 1964, 1965, 1987 by The Lockman Foundation. Used by permission. www.lockman.org

Scripture quotations marked (NASB) taken from the New American Standard Bible®, Copyright © 1960, 1962, 1963, 1968, 1971, 1972, 1973, 1975, 1977, 1995 by The Lockman Foundation. Used by permission. www.Lockman.org

Scripture quotations marked (NIV) are taken from the Holy Bible, New International Version®, NIV®. Copyright © 1973, 1978, 1984, 2011 by Biblica Inc.® Used by permission. All rights reserved

Scripture quotations marked "Phillips" or (PHILLIPS) are taken from The New Testament in Modern English, copyright © 1958, 1959, 1960 J.B. Phillips and 1947, 1952, 1955, 1957 The Macmillian Company, New York. Used by permission. All rights reserved.

TABLE OF CONTENTS

Introduction

It is almost impossible to write a book about a scriptural treatment of money-related matters without it stirring controversy. Unless we see the scriptures clearly by understanding how Jesus has taught it, it is easy for the unbelieving heart to misunderstand the language of scripture concerning God's nature and His riches. Submission to the Lord Jesus involves re-reading of the bible so that in the explanations of Jesus, He destroys satan's power to blind our understanding to the truth of scripture. Satan's power is the access to man's mind through false doctrine and unbelief concerning God's true nature. There are those who do not trust Jesus' explanation of God's riches, power and majesty and there are some that do. Our writings strengthen covetousness or establish our readers in contentment. Therefore, depending on the persuasion of the readers, some will find the teaching in this book controversial.

This book is not written so that the writer of the book can gain from you financially. It is written in the hope that the saint might know of the rich fruit of generosity that God has already placed in His saints. We write in the hope that the saint resolves that God should not be robbed of the pleasure of seeing His nature at work in His saints. We anticipate that many would catch on to the nature of God's generosity already contained within us in the New Birth.

The saint should not be enticed away from the simplicity that is in Christ. It is our prayer that in these pages your faith is helped to see God's riches in His saints. The revelation of Jesus is going forth throughout the earth with clarity and great power.

Kent, 2018.

1

Heed the warning of the Apostles

Materialism appears innocent and comes across as commonsensical. Its confession is "I am rich, and increased with goods, and have need of nothing". At its core, it assumes that God's riches are our material acquisitions and possessions. It is persuaded that the result of obedience is more material possessions.

On the other hand, legalism sees salvation as God rewarding me for my gift of good works to Him. It assumes that man initiates the giving-cycle and that God is obligated by our good works to give to man the harvest of salvation. Seen for what it is, materialism is the greatest "gift" of unbelief and selfishness and its first-born child is legalism. It is deception of the highest order to refuse to embrace the child (legalism) while preaching the mother (materialism). The revelation of Jesus destroys these two ideas that are the chief work of satan in the human heart.

Paul's words to the Philippians:

18. For many walk, of whom I have told you often, and now tell you even weeping, that they are the enemies of the cross of Christ:19. Whose end is destruction, whose God is their belly, and whose glory is in their shame, who mind earthly things.

Philippians 3:18 - 19

Paul wept about the grip of materialism which corrupts the message of ministers until their doctrine makes them "enemies of the cross of

Christ."

Their words choke the riches of the word from coming forth spiritual growth in the saints, for only the sincere milk of God's word brings spiritual growth.

2

Seed to the Sower

There's a lot for us to learn today from Paul's explanation of the grace of God seen in the Macedonian saints.

5. And this they did, not as we hoped, but first gave their own selves to the Lord, and unto us by the will of God.
2 Corinthians 8:5

We often tell sinners to give themselves to the Lord or "give your life to Christ." That is impossible. The sinner has no life to give to Christ. It is the saint that receives Christ as life and subsequently shows spiritual growth by giving their "own selves to the Lord." The foremost way you measure your understanding of the grace of the Lord Jesus is seen in that you first give your "own selves to the Lord." All else that we recognize as giving flows from this singular fact that you give youself to the Lord. The lifestyle of giving in the saint is "first give yourself to the Lord."

Then, you give yourself to the elders of the local assembly.

As a consequence, you give to other saints as a work of your faith and your expression of a life that is given to the Lord.

1 Moreover, brethren, we do you to wit of the grace of God bestowed on the churches of Macedonia; 2 how that in a great trial of affliction, the abundance of their joy and their deep poverty abounded unto the riches of their liberality.
2 Corinthians 8:1-2

Paul instructed the financially well-off Corinthians on their need to know "the grace of God bestowed on the churches of Macedonia." The saints at Jerusalem were in dire circumstances, the Macedonian saints in deep poverty, while the saints at Corinth were well off. This "grace of God" bestowed on the churches of Macedonia was independent of their finances. He doesn't tell the Corinthians to see their financial power as proof of the grace of God. He also doesn't tell them to see the deep poverty of the Macedonians as the grace of God. Whereas possessing financial power isn't God's grace, "first give yourself to the Lord" and liberality is.

What riches did God give the Macedonians?

The riches that God gave to the Macedonians is His nature in them expressed to others as the riches of liberality. The big difference between a saint and an unbeliever is that the saint has God's nature. This is the "much more" that the saint possesses. Although some saints don't like it, there is nothing that qualifies the saint to have more material things than the unbeliever.

While the book of Acts shows that the saints at Jerusalem had a model for giving (see Acts 4:34-35), that model did not stop them from needing financial support from others (see 1 Corinthians 16:1-3, Acts 11:29-30). The saints at Macedonia as well as other saints had to come to their aid. Why the change in fortune for the saints at Jerusalem? It wasn't that God switched from giving material riches directly to the saints at Judea to giving them indirectly through others. A combination of famine and persecution dried up their financial supply. The fact is that men operate the finances of the earth in ways that cause finances to go up and down. The financial system is earthly and man-made. Through His nature in us, God gives the saints His life as the giving heart. It is man that gives or withholds money.

Paul showed that the grace bestowed on the Macedonians and the grace of the Lord Jesus Christ are one and the same.

9 For ye know the grace of our Lord Jesus Christ, that, though he was rich, yet for your sakes he became poor, that ye through his poverty might be rich.
2 Corinthians 8:9

Paul's "he became poor, that ye through his poverty might be rich" is his restatement of his earlier point, "he hath made him to be sin for us, who knew no sin; that we might be made the righteousness of God in him" (see 2 Corinthians 5:21). The one made the righteousness of God in Him has been made rich. Jesus is God manifest in flesh. The very act of God manifesting in human flesh is poverty. By the same logic, becoming like him by believing in His resurrection from the dead makes us rich. Christ is the wealth of the saint. He is God's riches in us.

What is the grace of the Lord Jesus Christ?

The grace of the Lord Jesus Christ is the sacrificial giving of His life in order to reverse our death, which Paul referred to as poverty. The grace of the Lord Jesus Christ is not perishable things like silver and gold. It is not material. It is the life of sacrifice.

Did God give material resources to the Macedonians so that the Macedonians can in turn give it to the saints at Jerusalem?

The answer to that question has many ramifications.

The Macedonians were in "deep poverty", which means deep financial trouble (see 2 Corinthians 9:2). To say God gave them material resources would be to affirm that God was unable to get the saints at Jerusalem and the Macedonians out of deep poverty.

On the other hand, whatever God had given to the Macedonians is exactly what He had given to the Lord Jesus. Did God give money to the Lord Jesus so that we could be made rich (or righteous) in Him? Peter answers, "Forasmuch as ye know that ye were not redeemed with corruptible things, as silver and gold, from your vain conversation received by tradition from your fathers; But with the precious blood of Christ, as of a lamb without blemish and without spot" (see 1 Peter 1:18 - 19). No, God did not give material resources to the Macedonians so that the Macedonians could then give it to the saints in Judea. Think about it, why would God not directly give the material resources to those saints whose lives depended on it in the first place?

The Corinthians' recognition of the grace of God bestowed on the churches of Macedonia, would cause them to first give their "own selves to the Lord" and abound in liberality as a consequence. It was giving that God gave to the Macedonians (and to you too in Christ).

Paul later told these Corinthians about God giving seed to the sower:

10 Now he that ministereth seed to the sower both minister bread for your food, and multiply your seed sown, and increase the fruits of your righteousness;
2 Corinthians 9:10

What bread does God give for food?

Jesus had said, "the bread of God is he which cometh down from heaven, and giveth life unto the world" (see John 6:33). According to Jesus, the bread that God gives is Jesus as the bread that gives His life for men. "My Father giveth you the true bread from heaven" (see John 6:32). God has given us the sacrifice of His Son.

What does God minister to the sower?

Seed.

In Jesus' parable of the sower, the seed is the word of God. God's word is the seed of life that produces God's kingdom in men (see Mark 4:14, Matthew 13:18-19).

Peter says that we are born again by the incorruptible seed of God's word planted in our hearts (see 1 Peter 1:23). God's seed in us would mean that His heredity is ours. Through the gospel, the essence of

God's characteristics and traits have been reproduced in us. We have His DNA.

The seed of Abraham, the seed of David and the seed of the woman is now the seed of God in us (see Galatians 3:16, Romans 1:3-4, Genesis 3:15).

Truly, it is God that ministers seed to the sower.

Jesus is the seed that God plants into us as God's farm (see 1 Corinthians 3:9). Paul plants and other Ministers water that seed (see 1 Corinthians 3:6-11). This is how God sows Himself into us so as to bring forth His life in the earth.

In the previous verse, Paul had referred to this "seed to the sower" as "all grace abound toward you" (see 2 Corinthians 9:8). Thus far (in 2 Corinthians 8), Paul's example of the grace of giving had been the Lord Jesus and the Macedonians (see 2 Corinthians 8:1,9). The Lord and the Macedonians show that the "seed" evidences itself in a sacrificial life that gave itself to the Lord once and for all and to others continually. God's "seed to the sower" is sacrificial living which first gives itself to God and from that gives for the good of others. Paul was assuring the Corinthians that the same ability by which the Macedonians had given was already at work in the Corinthians. God's seed to the sower is the seed of God which is the giving heart.

This "seed to the sower" is "the abundance of their joy" (see 2 Corinthians 8:2) seen in the Macedonians' giving, which would be expressed as the cheerful giving of the saints in Corinth (see 2 Corinthians 9:6). Therefore, cheerful giving is God's seed which He has given to the saints. It is up to the saints to act on this as liberal distribution unto others (see 2 Corinthians 9:13). The same sacrificial life in the Son has been given to us as His gift in us and through us to our world. God gives the giving heart.

For clarity, the seed that God gave to the Corinthians wasn't material riches that the Corinthians could then give to the other saints. God doesn't play favorites by giving directly to some saints and then leaving all other saints at the mercy of those saints. The idea of God giving directly to one saint and only being able to give indirectly to another saint in need through the one He gave directly to does not present God as we have seen Him in Christ. The seed that God has given to each saint is the giving heart. However, each saint doesn't equally respond by giving themselves to the Lord nor does each saint have the same favorable financial situation. The lesson we learn together with the Corinthians from the Macedonians is that whether in deep poverty or great abundance, each saint is to practice cheerful giving as an end in itself.

12. For if there be first a willing mind, it is accepted according to that a man hath, and not according to that he hath not
2 Corinthians 8:12

Although Paul used the giving of the Macedonians to teach sacrificial giving, he establishes that giving from what we have is also grace-giving. The amount given by the Macedonians was small but the sacrificial nature of it turned it into a thing of marvel. A big amount given out of manipulation, guilt or covetousness is an investment into fear and greed. It isn't a "sacrifice acceptable", for it is not given according to our heredity in Christ. Our giving is a sacrifice because it comes from a free will and not because of the amount.

3

God's Riches

Although prayer is directed towards God, our words in prayer reveal to us what we think of God. We pray according to how we see God and, how we see ourselves in Him.

The riches of the glory of His inheritance

18. The eyes of your understanding being enlightened; that ye may know what is the hope of his calling, and what the riches of the glory of his inheritance in the saints, 19. And what is the exceeding greatness of his power to us-ward who believe, according to the working of his mighty power,
Ephesians 1:18 – 19

Saints do not pray anyhow but on God's terms, using His words, for God who is a spirit has given us His view of how He wants us praying.

In the God-given words that Paul used in his prayers, we find the answer to the question, "how great is God's power that works in us?"

Paul's prayer that we might know "the riches of the glory of his inheritance in the saints" challenges us to see riches from God's perspective and not from that of the natural man. For example, he doesn't pray for God to give us riches, instead he starts on the basis that the saint already has the riches of God but needs to have his or her recognition energised so as to acknowledge that fact – to know it better.

We understand God by His revelation of Himself in Christ – not by our feelings or experiences.

The word translated "enlightened" is from the Greek word that means "to cause to become clear to all, to render evident, to give light, to shine, to bring to light". Paul's prayer amplifies the psalmist's words, "Open thou mine eyes, that I may behold wondrous things out of thy law" (see Psalm 119:18). It is not the Word that needs to change, it is our vision of its message. We are to re-read the timeless message found in Genesis to Malachi with eyes that see God's big activity by His spirit in the saint. We are to have revelation of this spirit, which is His gift to us.

It is the Lamb that opens our eyes to see "wondrous things out of thy law." After the Lamb had opened their understanding to scriptures, the disciples said, "did not our heart burn within us, while he talked with us by the way, and while he opened to us the scriptures?" (see Luke 24:32). Remove the Lamb and the book remains closed. This burning of heart is the Lamb opening our understanding to see that the logic and message of God is the sufferings of Christ and the glories to follow that suffering. He (the Lamb) opened their understanding so that they might understand that the message of the book is about the victory of God through the Lamb.

Paul's "riches of the glory of his inheritance in the saints" shows us that God glories in His saints. We pray so that the saint may see himself or herself as the measure of God's wealth. The saint can confidently say, "the riches of God live here." We are to know that God, by the act of salvation, has made each saint rich.

The power of powerful power

Scholars have pointed out that Paul's prayer in Ephesians 1:19 contain the strongest concentration, in all of God's word, of an array of words describing power or a variant of it. We have four different words for power in a single sentence! This is an overdose of power.

The NASB states it this way:

and what is the surpassing greatness of His power toward us who believe. These are in accordance with the working of the strength of His might
Ephesians 1:19 (NASB)

The word that has been translated "exceeding" in the KJV, is the Greek word huperballo, made up of huper and ballo. Huper means above and beyond all else, while ballo means to throw or hurl. Together huper and ballo describe an archer who pulls back on his bow and releases his arrow, he overshoots, overreaches and surpasses his goal or target. Thus, the word has been translated "surpassing" in the NASB. It is throwing over and beyond anything. It is like the English hyperbole. Paul is saying that God went too far in producing a saint.

The word translated "greatness" means huge or vast in dimension, extent or any category. The riches of salvation are beyond human ability to measure.

The word translated "power" in "the exceeding greatness of his power" is the Greek word dunamis, which is His divine power given us to accomplish all that pertains to life and godliness (see 2 Peter 1:3). This is the power that accomplishes the Christian life. This word has been translated as strength in "and his countenance was as the sun shineth in his strength" (see Revelation 1:16). That's like the power of the sun - nuclear power. Dunamis is also used to describe the power that is inherent in the essential nature of a thing. As an example, the power in a tsunami is described as dunamis because it is power so strong that it simply cannot be resisted or defeated. It is inherent or self-generating power that accomplishes a task. This is power associated with the spirit we received in the New Birth.

The Greek word energeia, is derived from two words en and ergon. En means inside something or someone, while ergon means work. So energeia is God's working inside His saints. This word means "never idle or inactive." It is zealous labour or operative power. It describes that which is always effective. It is the arrival of God into a man in salvation with the same working of God that was seen in the resurrection of Jesus.

The Greek word ischus, which is translated "mighty" in the KJV is a word that describes visible or manifested power which puts one's strength to clear use. It is ultimate power, a show of force or ability that overcomes resistance. Paul explained this as God displaying His strength in resurrection – He raised us from spiritual death and lifted us with Christ all the way to the throne! Ischus power and dunamis power are linked (see Ephesians 2:4-6).

The Greek word kratos, which is translated "power" in "the working of his mighty power" is a different word that means endowed power or ability to express resident power. It is power associated with kings who rule and dominate.

Taken together, these various words for power paint a picture of the highest form of power that is overshooting and irresistible in us because we have believed the gospel. The Lord has used these words to reveal that this power, that originates only from God and is the greatest manifestation of power that this universe has been exposed to, is resident in each saint. No power has ever matched the power that God used to produce a saint. The only power like that which resides in the saint and which God used to produce a saint is that phenomenal power seen in Christ's resurrection.

The exceeding greatness of God's power is towards us or into us who believe.

Jeremiah prophesied of this exceeding power when he said, "Ah Lord GOD! behold, thou hast made the heaven and the earth by thy great power and stretched out arm, and there is nothing too hard for thee:" (see Jeremiah 32:17). God's power within each saint is beyond that used to make the heaven and the earth. God's proof that there is nothing too hard for Him is that He produced a saint! We are to understand better the power of the powerful power of God's power in the saint.

For we are his workmanship, created in Christ Jesus unto good works, which God hath before ordained that we should walk in them.
Ephesians 2:10

God wants His capacity measured by His work seen in His man in Christ. The degree of power that God has displayed in making the saint His workmanship means that the man in Christ is a far closer approximation of the boundaries of God's power than the first man in Adam was or ever could be. You could say that God created the earth and the heavens as His own dress-rehearsal to show man the bounds He would exceed in making the saint. In Genesis 1, Moses described the exercise of this power in parable form. The true genesis is seen in Christ.

It is the exceeding greatness of God's power that Paul describes when he speaks of "God, who is rich in mercy, for his great love wherewith he loved us," (see Ephesians 2:4). The riches conveyed by God, who is rich in mercy are the saints.

4. But God, who is rich in mercy, for his great love wherewith he loved us, 5. Even when we were dead in sins, hath quickened us together with Christ, (by grace ye are saved;) 6. And hath raised us up together, and made us sit together in heavenly places in Christ Jesus:
Ephesians 2:4 - 7

Exceeding means "going well beyond." God's act of raising us from the dead together with Christ Jesus surpassed every other use of power recorded in the bible. God's saving mercy is His power at maximum strength.

The chief achievement of God's mercy was the resurrection of Jesus. We trace out God's power by observing the saint. The riches of God is His power that quickened us together with Christ and raised us up with Him when we were dead in sins. Although, we like to refer to the empty grave as the proof of Jesus' resurrection, Paul says that God's workmanship is not the grave but the man totally recreated in Christ Jesus. That new man is the demonstration of the riches of His grace. The man in Christ is the exceeding greatness of God's resurrection power. This means that the New Birth, which has been given to all that believe the gospel, is God's power flaunted.

All "the working of his mighty power" produced the New Birth within the saint in Ephesians 2:5-7. The saint is the house of the surpassing greatness of divine power.

Why does the saint need to see this?

It is for the saint to recognize God's grace and mercy as the great expressions of His riches and power in the saint. We do not measure God's glory any other way.

Paul told the saints at Philippi, "I can do all things through Christ which strengtheneth me" (see Philippians 4:13). The expression "I can do" is ischuo, a variant of ischus. While "strengtheneth" in "which strengtheneth me" is dunamis.

What did Paul use that ischus, I-can-do power and that dunamis, I-am-strong power for?

The context is in the surrounding verses. "I know both how to be abased, and I know how to abound: everywhere and in all things I am instructed both to be full and to be hungry, both to abound and to suffer need" (see Philippians 4:12).

Paul used ischus and dunamis power to stay at rest on his inside independent of supply or lack on the outside. We war against the flesh and not against men, governments or earthly kingdoms. We wage war on the flesh and the works of the flesh. The working of God's mighty power kept Paul free of anxiety and covetousness when no one supported him in his hour of need. This is the measure of the riches of God's inheritance in the saints.

The ischus and dunamis power that we are strengthened with in the Lord is not power to take over governments or attain political office. We have been led by the spirit out of the flesh into salvation. Our fight is not against flesh and blood (see Ephesians 6:12). We are the riches of that mighty Lamb.

16 That he would grant you, according to the riches of his glory, to be strengthened with might by his Spirit in the inner man;
Ephesians 3:16

"His Spirit in the inner man" is the riches and power of God in us. The "riches of His glory" is strengthening with kratos power by His spirit in the inner man.

Thus, God's riches and His power are one and the same thing. When we talk of the riches of God, we are examining the power of God.

The Greek word translated strengthened in "strengthened with might" is krataioo (a variant of kratos). He prays that they be strengthened with kratos. This is how God's power works in the saint.

Why this strengthening?

This is so that the saint is able to comprehend with all saints what is the breadth, and length, and depth, and height; And to know the love of Christ, which passeth knowledge, that ye might be filled with all the fulness of God (see Ephesians 3:18-19).

The word translated comprehend in "comprehend with all saints" is one which means to seize, catch or lay hold of with the mind. This is understanding.

This strength is for comprehending the fullness of God in His saints by His spirit in them! The riches of God are seen in His spirit in us, which is the work of God's love in Christ. The riches of His glory are the spiritual comprehension of what God has done.

Echoes from the holy scriptures

Although, Moses had seen the wealth and splendour of Egypt and he had also seen the staggering miracles associated with Israel's deliverance from Egypt, Yet, after all that he still asked God, "show me your glory" (see Exodus 33:18). Thus, Moses recognised that the glory of God was other than the wealth and riches of kings or even miracles. Isaiah saw that glory, for he said, "the whole earth is full of his glory" (see Isaiah 6:3). Isaiah described that glory as "Lo, this hath touched thy lips; and thine iniquity is taken away, and thy sin purged" (see Isaiah 6:7). The glory of God that Isaiah saw is the Lord as the cleanser and cleansing of sins who purifies the heart of those who believe. The Lord Jesus said, "these things said Esaias, when he saw his glory, and spake of him" (see John 12:41). Thus, the glory of the Lord is a person – Christ! Christ's work in purifying the heart of the believer is glory and riches. The eyes of the saints opened to see the riches of glory would be the saint seeing Christ as the riches of the purging of sins and not the giving of material riches.

Paul speaks of the riches of the glory of His inheritance in the saints (see Ephesians 1:18). The riches of the glory cannot mean that material riches exist inside the saints in spiritual form. The "riches of glory" is God supplying His spirit to us in the New Birth as proof of the riches of the purging of sins. God's spirit in us is His riches in us. According to Paul's revelation, salvation is God's riches in the saint by His spirit in them.

The riches of their liberality

1. Moreover, brethren, we do you to wit of the grace of God bestowed on the churches of Macedonia; 2. How that in a great trial of affliction the abundance of their joy and their deep poverty abounded unto the riches of their liberality.
2 Corinthians 8:1 - 2

The grace God gave the churches of Macedonia is the nature of God in Christ which Paul referred to as the grace of our Lord Jesus. That grace is the power of the Lord to lay down His life in sacrificial death for the saints. The saints then express that power as "the riches of their liberality."

The riches of God's grace, the exceeding greatness of God's power and the riches of the liberality of the saints are one and the same thing.

God power in the earth today is the riches of the liberality of the saints. The vast power that was operative in the Lord and energizing liberality in the Macedonians is resident in each saint today. The powerful power of God possessed in Christ is not the power to reign over others, take over cities or to dominate people. It is the power to serve others even when it is not convenient.

The riches of the liberality is the height of God's power showcased in His saints, who are His workmanship. "The riches of their liberality" means that we are to see the liberality of saints as riches. "The riches of their liberality" refer to the freedom with which the Macedonians had given to others when it was obvious that these Macedonians did not have material abundance.

In the writings of the prophets, God prophesied of His riches, while in the epistles, God explains His riches so that we can pay attention to what it is and recognize those riches in us.

12. Now if the fall of them be the riches of the world, and the diminishing of them the riches of the Gentiles; how much more their fulness?
Romans 11:12

Paul confirms the fulfilment of Isaiah's "ye shall eat the riches of the Gentiles" (see Isaiah 61:6).

Isaiah explained the eating the "riches of the gentiles" as "therefore in their land they shall possess the double" (see Isaiah 61:7). The double is the double portion, which refers to the inheritance of the first born. This is the inheritance of everlasting joy, which is everlasting salvation. So, the riches of the gentiles is their everlasting salvation.

10. I will greatly rejoice in the LORD, my soul shall be joyful in my God; for he hath clothed me with the garments of salvation, he hath covered me with the robe of righteousness, as a bridegroom decketh himself with ornaments, and as a bride adorneth herself with her jewels.
Isaiah 61:10

Furthermore, Isaiah explained the figure of speech "riches of the gentiles" as clothes, robes, decking with ornaments and adorning with jewels. These are measures of wealth. In Isaiah's prophecy, he wasn't speaking of material riches but God's riches, for the clothes are the garments of salvation and the robe is the robe of righteousness as God's gift. He also described salvation as ornaments and the adorning of jewels. The riches of the gentiles describe salvation as God's true riches supplied to the non-Jews by Christ's resurrection.

The "riches of the gentiles" means that the resurrection of Christ is the supply of salvation to the gentiles. Those gentiles that believe the gospel receive salvation as riches from God, while those that reject it do not have God's riches. We see salvation as riches. The gentile's reception of God's supply of salvation is the riches of the gentiles. This agrees with the prophet's "and the Gentiles shall come to thy light, and kings to the brightness of thy rising" (see Isaiah 60:3).

7. In whom we have redemption through his blood, the forgiveness of sins, according to the riches of his grace;
Ephesians 1:7

"The riches of his grace" means that God wants the saint to recognise God's grace as His riches. God's riches is His work in supplying forgiveness. The forgiveness of sins is the riches of His grace. The saint who has received forgiveness from God has received His riches.

26 Esteeming the reproach of Christ greater riches than the treasures in Egypt: for he had respect unto the recompence of the reward.
Hebrews 11:26

Moses recognised the reproach of Christ as riches - even greater riches than the treasures of Egypt. The reproach of Christ refers to Moses living a life of sacrifice in service to Israel on account of God's promise of salvation. Thus, living sacrificially for others from a revelation of Christ is riches. We esteem a life of sacrifice as true riches on account of the gospel.

17. Charge them that are rich in this world, that they be not highminded, nor trust in uncertain riches, but in the living God, who giveth us richly all things to enjoy;
1 Timothy 6:17

Although, Paul also referred to money and similar natural resources as riches, when he did so, he qualified the nature of those riches by referring to them as uncertain riches. The word translated "uncertain" is a Greek word that means that which vanishes. This means that material wealth fades - material riches are not enduring.

33 O the depth of the riches both of the wisdom and knowledge of God! how unsearchable are his judgments, and his ways past finding out!
Romans 11:33

Paul spoke of the riches of God's wisdom. He means that wisdom (the knowledge of His salvation) is riches.

4 Or despisest thou the riches of his goodness and forbearance and longsuffering; not knowing that the goodness of God leadeth thee to repentance?
Romans 2:4

In the NIV it reads, "kindness, forbearance and patience." The riches of goodness and forbearance and longsuffering are the riches of kindness, forbearance and patience. Thus, kindness, goodness, forbearance, patience and longsuffering are God's riches. By implication, God's riches is His works. The saint that walks in the spirit by the fruit of the spirit walks in the riches of God.

7 That in the ages to come he might shew the exceeding riches of his grace in his kindness toward us through Christ Jesus.
Ephesians 2:7

God's kindness is the riches of His grace given to us in Christ.

Thus far, God's "riches" is not material wealth but the work of that spirit that God has dealt to each saint in Christ.

Paul affirms the truth of the riches of glory to the Philippians:

19. But my God shall supply all your need according to his riches in glory by Christ Jesus.
Philippians 4:19

Paul told the Philippian saints who were the chief supporters of Paul's ministry that God supplies their need by Christ. Interestingly, he does not say, "my God shall supply your need because you have given to me." He assures them that God's riches is "by Christ Jesus." Thus, Christ is God's currency of supply. God is not looking for your seed. He has given us Christ as His seed sown into our hearts by the gospel. Christ is God's riches in us today. God's riches in the saint is His nature in them, which is the giving heart. The liberality of the saints is riches. God had used His riches in the Macedonians to supply the material need of others (see 2 Corinthians 8:2).

In the same way that education, marriage and food are not exclusive to saints, money or material riches is not God's gift in Christ.

Eat the good of the land

Although the language used to express God's riches make it appear material, the prophets did not prophesy material riches.

Here is a sample ancient prophecy of scripture:

18. Come now, and let us reason together, saith the LORD: though your sins be as scarlet, they shall be as white as snow; though they be red like crimson, they shall be as wool. 19. If ye be willing and obedient, ye shall eat the good of the land: 20. But if ye refuse and rebel, ye shall be devoured with the sword: for the mouth of the LORD hath spoken it.
Isaiah 1:18 – 20

The word translated "willing" is a word that refers to man's choice to heed the utterance of the prophet rather than disregard it. The word translated "obedient" refers to believing the utterances in those ancient prophecies.

What was the utterance? These are the words of the prophet, "though your sins be as scarlet, they shall be as white as snow; though they be red like crimson, they shall be as wool." It is God cleansing a man from sins that is the good of the land. The good of the land is not business empires, diamonds, careers or business deals but God's supply of cleansing. Paul calls this cleansing from sin the riches of His grace (see Ephesians 1:7). Therefore, to eat the good of the land is to receive the riches of the land, which is figurative language for receiving the riches of cleansing, which is the forgiveness of sins. The prophet's gospel assurance is "though they be red like crimson, they shall be as wool" (see Isaiah 1:18).

The one who receives the riches of cleansing is said to be together with Him in that the believing one joins God in His work, not so as to do any work but to be the recipient of the report that God has done His. He has cleansed our sins by the sacrifice of His Son. We have received the riches of His grace by faith in Christ.

This prophecy of eating the good of the land was God encouraging men from ancient times to believe God's promise that He would cleanse man's sins. In that prophecy, God's action of cleansing is the good of the land, which is true riches. God has given the good of the land in the sacrifice of Christ. It is no longer a promise. The man who believes the gospel has eaten the good of the land. He has received the riches of cleansing.

The prophet's words, "but if ye refuse and rebel, ye shall be devoured with the sword" affirms the judgment inherent in refusing God's riches of cleansing. Such a person is without God's riches by choice and is poor, wretched and miserable even if that person abounds in material riches.

4

The Two-Fold Sacrifice

2. As newborn babes, desire the sincere milk of the word, that ye may grow thereby: 3. If so be ye have tasted that the Lord is gracious.
1 Peter 2:2-3

It is to be observed that Peter does not call these saints new born babes for there are no babes in Christ. The man in Christ is perfect in status, standing and nature; this is the work of God in those that have believed the gospel. The expression, "that ye may grow thereby" does not mean that men grow into salvation – salvation isn't a result of spiritual growth. Peter speaks to those who are already in Christ. They are to grow in that salvation already possessed. However, those already made perfect in Christ are often undeveloped in conduct. This deficiency in understanding and conduct is described as "like new born babes".

The milk of the word is the knowledge of the graciousness of the Lord.

The power of God's grace can be cooperated with by receiving the milk of God's word. He is saying to all saints, "milk is powerful for growth". There is no saint who is beyond spiritual growth.

Milk does not mean the same thing everywhere in scripture.

For example, Paul's "I have fed you with milk, and not with meat" (see 1 Corinthians 3:2), was a description of his care for them in the way that he ministered to them. The point is easier to see in the NASB that says, "I gave you milk to drink, not solid food". The expression, "I have fed you with milk, and not with meat" is a figure of speech. It wasn't what he said; it was how he said it. It is a reference to his mode of teaching on account of how those saints were ready to receive ministry. Milk in "I have fed you with milk, and not with meat", does not refer to the truth itself. Paul's point is seen in the way the book of Corinthians is written. He taught them with a lot of parables. He tailored how he presented the truth to a format that suited them. Interestingly, the Corinthian passage shows that Paul measured spiritual growth by how ready people were to receive spiritual truth and to walk in love towards others – not the size of their earrings, dress length or lack of a good dress sense couched as spirituality.

Peter's term "milk of the word" doesn't mean that the truth of God's word varies in quality with some portions of God's word being milk and other portions to be treated as meat. Peter's "milk of the word" means that gospel truth, which is the knowledge of the sacrifice of Christ, is nutritious for spiritual growth. The saint should continue to hear the truth of Christ's sacrifice without getting weary. There is danger inherent in weariness, for with weariness comes stagnation. The saint that doesn't fervently feed on the truth of God's word is already feeding from anti-Christian streams – such a saint is regressing spiritually.

Peter also says, "But grow in grace, and in the knowledge of our Lord and Saviour Jesus Christ" (see 2 Peter 3:18). He doesn't want the saint to be nonchalant about hearing the truth of the grace of the Lord Jesus as it is potent to produce spiritual growth when we understand its message. Peter's "milk of the word" is the knowledge of the grace of our Lord. Grace is the knowledge of our Lord Jesus Christ. This is meat for growth. Thus, Peter's "milk of the word" is meat for spiritual growth.

Peter would later show that this spiritual growth is seen in ministering to other saints.

4. To whom coming, as unto a living stone, disallowed indeed of men, but chosen of God, and precious,
1 Peter 2:4

We came to Jesus as the living stone. Jesus is God's only foundation for salvation. We came to Him by believing the news of His sacrifice for our sins.

5. Ye also, as lively stones, are built up a spiritual house, an holy priesthood, to offer up spiritual sacrifices, acceptable to God by Jesus Christ.
1 Peter 2:5

Once we believe the gospel, we do not only see Jesus as the living stone, we acknowledge that we also are lively stones – we are a spiritual house. Our identity as lively stones mean that as a holy nation of priests, each saint offers up spiritual sacrifices. God supplied Christ as sacrifice for our sins. In the bible, God is never the beneficiary of sacrifice. God did not ask for man's sacrifices to Him (see Hebrews 10:5-6, Micah 6:6-8, Psalm 40:6). God is not interested in sacrifices from man to Him.

18. But I have all, and abound: I am full, having received of Epaphroditus the things which were sent from you, an odour of a sweet smell, a sacrifice acceptable, wellpleasing to God.
Philippians 4:18

Paul received the gifts given to him by the Philippians as a sweet-smelling sacrifice. It pleased God but it was received by Paul. It is other men who live amongst us that need our sacrifices. When we show others mercy, we are offering up sacrifices they can benefit from. The slant of scriptures is that we offer sacrifices to those among us who need it. God's view is "I do not need it!" The sacrifice to offer is "learn to do well; seek judgment, relieve the oppressed, judge the fatherless, plead for the widow" (see Isaiah 1:11,13,18).

2. And walk in love, as Christ also hath loved us, and hath given himself for us an offering and a sacrifice to God for a sweetsmelling savour.
Ephesians 5:2

The Message translation says, "He didn't love in order to get something from us but to give everything of himself to us. Love like that." Our love walk towards other saints is our spiritual sacrifice. Our sacrifice is doing good to other saints. We present good works to men as our spiritual sacrifice for their edification. The "sacrifice to God" is His pleasure that we present that sacrifice to others as our reverence for God. We are not giving God any sacrifice. He doesn't need it from us to Him. We imitate Christ's love by recognizing that God has not desired sacrifices but that it pleases Him that we recognize that it is other men who live amongst us that need our sacrifices.

To "offer up spiritual sacrifices, acceptable to God by Jesus Christ" means that in Christ's sacrifice, we find a life of sacrifice for others.

9. But ye are a chosen generation, a royal priesthood, an holy nation, a peculiar people; that ye should shew forth the praises of him who hath called you out of darkness into his marvellous light:
1 Peter 2:9

Holiness is characteristic of each believer for it is the identity of the family of God. The whole nation of saints is holy. This means that there is no unholy saint. Holiness is God's choice of the man in Christ.

"The praises of Him" refer to God's works in Christ who gave Himself for our sins. Our showing forth His praises refers to our offering up spiritual sacrifices (see verse 5). Our sacrifice is the riches of good works. We present good works to men who benefit from it. We live sacrificially for that is the Lord's example. Showing forth the praises of Him is not a reference to having the best house, car or shoe in town. For example, rather than respond in malice towards brethren that offend we offer the spiritual sacrifice of walking in God's extravagant love (see 1 Peter 2:1). The sacrifice of Christ is the explanation of our spiritual sacrifice.

This is how Paul taught this two-fold sacrifice to the saints at Rome:

1. I beseech you therefore, brethren, by the mercies of God, that ye present your bodies a living sacrifice, holy, acceptable unto God, which is your reasonable service.
Romans 12:1

God's abundant mercy is the resurrection of Jesus Christ from the dead. "… according to his abundant mercy hath begotten us again unto a lively hope by the resurrection of Jesus Christ from the dead" (see 1 Peter 1:3). Therefore, those that have received the New Birth "have obtained mercy" (see 1 Peter 2:10). Thus, Paul's "the mercies of God" refers to his explanation, in the first 11 chapters of Romans, of what God had accomplished for us in Christ's sacrifice. The sacrifice of Christ is the mercy of God.

Now, he anticipates that the knowledge of God's mercies in Christ's sacrifice causes the saints to recognize that in that sacrifice, our bodies have been made holy unto the Lord and acceptable to God (see 1 Corinthians 6:19-20). That knowledge awakens in the saint "reasonable service."

The word translated "reasonable" in Romans 12:1 is the same word Peter has translated "word" in "sincere milk of the word". It is divine logic.

We are to renew our mind to the logic embedded in Christ's sacrifice by agreeing that Christ's sacrifice has changed the status of our body. In substance, the body remains mortal but in status it is now holy, acceptable to God and useful for service to other saints. You are presenting your body to your mind in that new light that the body of the saint is not unholy but holy. As a result, you continually offer up the spiritual sacrifice of a life of service to other saints because that is the logic of Christ's sacrifice. This is the renewal of the mind to God's logic.

The sacrifice of Christ produces a life of service in His saints.

I reason along with Paul in Romans until I see Christ's sacrifice as His service to me. In His service to me I see my service to others – my service shows His work in me. It shows my recognition of being made holy in him.

Christ our Passover

7 Purge out therefore the old leaven, that ye may be a new lump, as ye are unleavened. For even Christ our Passover is sacrificed for us:
1 Corinthians 5:7

Paul's teachings were his explanation of the holy scriptures (see Ephesians 3:3-4). He explains the Passover and the unleavened bread as referring to Christ and His saints! Unbelief wants to continue with the ritualistic eating of the Passover but he explains Christ as its fulfillment. The eyes of the saint's understanding need to be opened to see what the holy scriptures teach so clearly. The hope of God's call are those ancient promises contained in the holy scriptures and now fulfilled in Christ's sacrifice.

The Passover beautifully shows how God's mercy passed over the door so that death could not enter in (see Exodus 12). In Exodus, the blood on the door was symbolic of mercy suspending death's claim on the life of the first born. That Passover was the substance of things hoped for (a reference to God's word to save from destruction). It was not the physical food but the heart that believes the gospel (see Hebrews 11:28). It was not God that destroyed but another. God was saving from the "he that destroyed." Whereas, under the shadow in Exodus, some might have brought the Passover; in Christ's sacrifice, the Passover was for us but never brought by us. Paul's explanation that Christ is our Passover already sacrificed means that Jesus was the Passover that God has supplied for our benefit. God gave that sacrifice as His gift to us. We brought nothing but a believing heart.

What Moses wrote about the Passover, he wrote about Christ for Jesus said, "For had ye believed Moses, ye would have believed me: for he wrote of me" (see John 5: 46). Since Christ is our God-supplied Passover, we do not need to seek any Passover ordinance or ceremony. Instead, we recognize that the Lord Jesus is the fulfillment of the message taught through the Passover ordinance. In seeing the Lord as our Passover, we readily acknowledge that "ye are unleavened" - the unleavened bread is cleansing from sin by Christ's sacrifice. We are that unleavened bread. The feasts have been fulfilled in Christ and we are in Him.

The Passover was a reference to His body. He bore our sins on His own body so that by His stripes we were healed, which means we have the remission of all our sins (see 1 Peter 2:24).

The saint who celebrates or attaches any importance to the ordinance of Passover and similar feasts fails to recognize that those symbols were dark sayings pointing to the reality already possessed by the saint.

This is how Paul explains the cup of blessing:

16. The cup of blessing which we bless, is it not the communion of the blood of Christ? The bread which we break, is it not the communion of the body of Christ? 17. For we being many are one bread, and one body: for we are all partakers of that one bread.
1 Corinthians 10:16 - 17

Paul had identified Christ as the spiritual drink (see 1 Corinthians 10:4). Now he refers to "the cup of blessing, which we bless."

Notice how Paul picks his words.

The word translated "communion" means fellowship, which means supply which is received. The communion of the body of Christ means the supply of the body of Christ which we have received. This refers to the fact that we have found life in that we received Christ's offering of Himself. The bread that Paul is focusing the saints on is the communion of the body of Christ who is the true bread indeed.

Paul's big truth to the Corinthians is found in the words "we being many are one bread, and one body: for we are all partakers of that one bread". Paul declares that the bread is the fellowship of saints in Christ.

We are partakers of Christ who is the bread and have received Him as bread. Therefore, we are one bread with Him and with one another. Thus, the saint sees in Christ and the brotherhood of saints the fulfillment of the unleavened bread. We are one bread and one body. There is no other unleavened bread elsewhere. We look away from the ceremony of unleavened bread for we have learned its lesson in the sacrifice of Christ who gave Himself to us.

Since Jesus as bread describes His sacrifice, we as bread are transformed by His sacrifice to live the same way – we give ourselves in service to others. This is our sacrifice, which means service to others. Each saint lives sacrificially for other saints for each saint is one bread with Christ.

Paul illustrates this thought in chapter 11:

Corinthians via Colossians and Ephesians

23. For I have received of the Lord that which also I delivered unto you, That the Lord Jesus the same night in which he was betrayed took bread: 24. And when he had given thanks, he brake it, and said, Take, eat: this is my body, which is broken for you: this do in remembrance of me. 25. After the same manner also he took the cup, when he had supped, saying, This cup is the new testament in my blood: this do ye, as oft as ye drink it, in remembrance of me.
1 Corinthians 11:23 – 25

Paul faithfully replayed the commonly accepted tradition of what transpired in the Passover meal – this is recorded in the four gospels. It'll appear that Paul quoted Luke's account. The words closely correspond to Luke 22:19-20.

Prior to that last Passover meal, Jesus had explained that He was the bread from heaven that is eaten once and quenches hunger once and forever (see John 6:32-35). Jesus as bread is the giver of life. He said, "I am the living bread which came down from heaven: if any man eat of this bread, he shall live for ever: and the bread that I will give is my flesh, which I will give for the life of the world" (see John 6:51). Human hunger for deliverance from sin is quenched permanently.

Jesus explained what He meant by "the bread that I will give is my flesh" in these words "the words that I speak unto you, they are spirit, and they are life". Jesus is saying, "My body and my blood are hidden in My word." God has hidden the body and blood of Jesus in the Gospel message. When Jesus spoke of His blood and His flesh, He was referring to His spirit that makes alive. He used "blood", "body" and "flesh" to teach the truth of resurrection. In other words, it is what a man does with the truth of the resurrection that determines whether that man receives that "making alive" or not. The believing one receives life, while the doubter does not. His hearers tried to take His words about bread and body literally and so doing they missed His teaching (see John 6:60-66). It is the nature of parables that they keep the truth hidden from those with a hard heart. What Jesus said had nothing to do with bread from the oven or the biting of His literal flesh. We have eaten the body of Jesus as bread by believing the gospel message.

We do well to approach Corinthians via Colossians and Ephesians because in Colossians and Ephesians, Paul uses great plainness of speech. In Corinthians he could not speak unto them "as unto spiritual, but as unto carnal, even as unto babes in Christ" (see 1 Corinthians 3:1). In 1st Corinthians, his speech is not so plain.

16 Let no man therefore judge you in meat, or in drink, or in respect of an holyday, or of the new moon, or of the sabbath days: 17 Which are a shadow of things to come; but the body is of Christ.
Colossians 2:16-17

It is one word that has been translated "things to come" in "a shadow of things to come" (see Colossians 2:17). The word means doing something or suffering something. The text can be translated "shadow of the sacrifice to come". The Passover pointed to Christ's sacrifice.

The body is of Christ means Moses was teaching about Christ and that He is the reality that the feasts stood in place of and pointed to. The man that believes knows that there was nothing to any of the feasts and ordinances asides being teaching aids for those who couldn't believe God's promise. It is because the feasts are nothing more than teaching aids devoid of reality that Paul said to let no man judge you in meat, drink, holy feasts, new moons or Sabbath days. Therefore, Paul could not be judging the Corinthians concerning the eating or non-eating of the Passover (commonly referred to as "communion") for the ceremonies have never been needed by those that believe. Whatever special powers people attribute to the literal observance of those feasts today are man-made or doctrines of men. The man in Christ has received the sacrifice of Christ and cannot be judged by the observance or none observance of a shadow or symbol.

The doctrines of men attach powers to ordinances while veiling the mind from the reality in Christ. As a result, saints judge one another with respect to the bread and wine where the ordinance of Passover is concerned. Again, Jesus' words, "For had ye believed Moses, ye would have believed me: for he wrote of me" (see John 5:46).

Recall what Paul had taught the Ephesians:

having abolished in his flesh the enmity, even the law of commandments contained in ordinances; for to make in himself of twain one new man, so making peace;
Ephesians 2:15

Concerning the feasts, Paul told the Ephesians that Jesus has already abolished in his flesh the law of commandments contained in ordinances.

Abolish is a strong term. Jesus has personally abolished the keeping of the unleavened bread and Passover feasts and ceremonies together with its various ordinances. We should not re-instate the keeping of ordinances that Jesus has abolished.

In the light of his own teachings, Paul could not be putting the Corinthian saints back under the yoke of observing ordinances that have been abolished. He had already explained the reality of those ordinances in Christ.

He taught the Colossians:

If you then be risen with Christ, why as though living in the world are you subject to ordinances? (see Colossians 1:20).

The articles of the ordinance perish with the use (bread and wine).

Those who are risen with Christ are no longer subject to ordinances. We do not observe ceremonies that have been superseded by the death, burial, resurrection and indwelling of Jesus.

1 If ye then be risen with Christ, seek those things which are above, where Christ sitteth on the right hand of God. 2 Set your affection on things above, not on things on the earth.
Colossians 3:1-2

Some scholars refer to this "if" as the if of certainty. Its sense is better conveyed as "since you are risen with Christ".

Seek things above does not mean lift your gaze towards the skies. "Above" refers to the saint's sitting with Christ. Acknowledge and reason from the reality of being seated with Christ. It is yielding to the knowledge of Christ as the believer's reality. Don't look to ordinances, look to the fulfilment in that you are seated with Christ.

We keep the feast the Christian way

8 Therefore let us keep the feast, not with old leaven, neither with the leaven of malice and wickedness; but with the unleavened bread of sincerity and truth.
1 Corinthians 5:8

We keep the feast the Christian way by not attaching special powers to abolished ordinances or ceremonies, which are mere teaching aids, but by understanding that the Passover pointed to Christ's sacrifice while the unleavened bread pointed to innocence received as God's gift to us in Christ. The Christian way of keeping the feast is by recognizing that our Passover is a person. The Christian way is following the example of Jesus. We live for others. We let Christ's example shape our fellowship with men.

In 1 Corinthians 11, Paul is teaching the Corinthians the lesson behind what the Lord said during that Passover just before His death.

With bread in His hands, Jesus said, "Take, eat: this is my body, which is broken for you."

The man with a hardened heart of unbelief would look to the bread in Jesus' hands.

The man who sees the things of the spirit will not look to the bread from the bakery. He'll wait for the supply of that bread in the sacrifice of Christ. The bread in His hands was powerless. Jesus is the true bread from heaven. "This is my body which is broken for you" means "I am the reality. I give myself to you."

Paul is teaching the saints to remember that the Lord Jesus gave Himself to us all.

Why is Paul telling this to the Corinthians?

The Corinthians were not showing the Lord's death.

The Lord's death is the giving of Himself as sacrifice. We show that death by giving ourselves in the same spirit of sacrifice to our brethren "in remembrance of Him." We keep the feast by preferring our brethren and watching out for their welfare. When we do not live sacrificially for other saints we show selfishness. The cure is the sincere milk of the truth of Jesus' sacrifice. Without that sincere milk, we hinder our own spiritual growth.

We are unleavened bread. We as bread give ourselves just as He gave. This is not seen in our death but in our bearing one another's burden as we live for one another. We live to share with our brethren (see Galatians 6:2).

Here is what Paul was addressing:

21. For in eating every one taketh before other his own supper: and one is hungry, and another is drunken.
1 Corinthians 11:21

The immediate problem that Paul was addressing was "one is hungry, and another is drunken". There was selfishness in the Corinthian church. Selfish saints refused to share but rather overstuffed themselves to the point of drunkenness while fellow saints who were poor in their midst came to the love feast hungry and left hungry.

Paul was discussing the sacredness of giving to others like Christ gave Himself to us. Christ's example of sharing Himself with all causes us to give to other saints recognizing that He is alive in us today still giving Himself in our selfless love for other saints. That is the exceeding greatness of God's power at work in the saint.

Eateth and drinketh damnation to himself

29 For he that eateth and drinketh unworthily, eateth and drinketh damnation to himself, not discerning the Lord's body. 30 For this cause many are weak and sickly among you, and many sleep.
1 Corinthians 11:29-30

Notice that Paul does not say that the bread brings damnation. Loaves of bread proceed from bakeries and end up in the toilet. They have absolutely no spiritual attribute.

Also, Paul had earlier taught the Corinthians that food does not commend us to God! He said to the Corinthians, "neither am I better if I eat nor am I worse off if I do not eat" (see 1 Corinthians 8:8).

It is the saint that brings damnation upon himself by failing to discern the Lord's body. There is nothing inherent in the bread that brings about the damage. The bread did not become more dangerous; it was the people that became more divided.

John discusses the challenges of selfishness:

17 But whoso hath this world's good, and seeth his brother have need, and shutteth up his bowels of compassion from him, how dwelleth the love of God in him? 18 My little children, let us not love in word, neither in tongue; but in deed and in truth. 19 And hereby we know that we are of the truth, and shall assure our hearts before him. 20 For if our heart condemn us, God is greater than our heart, and knoweth all things. 21 Beloved, if our heart condemn us not, then have we confidence toward God.

1 John 3:17-21

John describes a scenario where one believer has this world's goods, notices another brother who lacks that which he has and rather than share, the brother that has the goods refuses to.

This shutting "up his bowels of compassion from him" is refusal to share with other saints that have need. God does not need or demand sacrifices, it is saints in need that benefit from it. To shut "up his bowels of compassion" is to refuse to offer up spiritual sacrifices.

The expression, "and shutteth up his bowels of compassion from him" means that the riches of compassion welled up within the believer who had material riches. God's exceeding great power wanted to show as the riches of liberality in the saint because that power is present in each saint. However, this Christian ignored the outflow of the riches of kindness that was reaching out towards the needy. The new nature was attempting to influence the born again to express the riches of liberality but this believer refused the flow of that power. He was preventing the power of God in him from producing the love walk.

By deliberately shutting up his bowels, he was waging war on God's purpose in the New Covenant. At that point his heart received condemnation, which registered in his life as loss of confidence. His confidence was gone. In Paul's language, we would say, "he bringeth damnation upon himself." The damnation is not imparted by "this world's goods". Damnation is the condemnation that shows up as a wounded conscience, a loss of confidence that comes from shutting up compassion from guiding one's conduct.

John has described what "damnation" is while Paul simply stated it.

The damnation is not imparted by the bread but by unbelief that manifests as lack of the love walk towards other saints. Unbelief administers damnation. It is our heart condemning us for not walking in love towards other saints.

There is danger in not discerning the Lord's body.

What do we discern in the Lord's body? We see the sacrificial giving of Himself as our example of not living for ourselves but for others too. I recognize that I am bread to be shared too.

The saints who overstuffed themselves to the point of drunkenness while fellow saints starved "shut up their bowels of compassion" by discarding the example seen in Christ. They failed to recognize that the starving saints were members of the same body and fellow heirs. Their mind had been entangled with selfishness because they had an unclear view of God.

What are the consequence of the saints "not discerning the Lord's body"?

Paul said, "For this cause many are weak and sickly among you, and many sleep".

Sleep refers to physical death.

Many were weak, sickly and dying prematurely among the saints and the saints were puzzled as to why. It was a mystery to them. Paul removed the mystery by explaining what was going on. It is likely that the Corinthians had asked Paul that question. Paul is now giving them the answer. He is showing that premature death is not mysterious. While superstitious saints glory in mysteries, saints who receive the word glory in clarity.

Paul wasn't saying that saints were weak, sickly and dying because of improper observation of a shadow.

Since Paul had said earlier that after their supper, "one is hungry and another drunken", these judgments (dire outcomes) could be two-fold:

The saints who were given to drunkenness were the ones needing to judge themselves of their excesses. They were walking in selfishness and excess. Their excesses exposed their bodies to sicknesses and diseases, which resulted in death.

The other logical position would be that those saints who were shamed and had none to share with them were hungry and destitute as a result of which they were sickly or died early. Malnutrition and other factors wiped them out. The wealthy saints had not shown the Lord's death; they had not lived sacrificially.

Wait for one another

33 Wherefore, my brethren, when ye come together to eat, tarry one for another.
1 Corinthians 11:33

Paul gave love's solution to the predicament of saints dying prematurely due to selfishness at Corinth. He gave a very practical solution: They were to wait for one another.

The very act of waiting would give expression to the riches of kindness which they all possess via the New Birth. Those who would have become drunk before now exercised more restraint to win the spirit's war against the flesh. Instead of "shutting up their bowels" they would express the riches of liberality, thus showing the Lord's death. There would be more sharing. This meant that all those who would have gone hungry would have something to eat. The mind does not receive damnation and the weakness and sickness leading to death would be held back.

Notice that he said, "when ye come together to eat, ..."

This meant that the Corinthians came together to eat. Eating together had a central place in the early church;

11 When he therefore was come up again, and had broken bread, and eaten, and talked a long while, even till break of day, so he departed.
Acts 20:11

After raising Eutychus from the dead, Paul broke bread, had a feast and preached up a storm. Paul raised Eutychus so that he could still minister the gospel for a long while afterwards. Thus, raising the dead was part of the service and not the end of the service. Eating was also part of the service. All they did centred around the preaching of God's word.

Paul used a long-winded way to say to the Corinthians that the solution to the tragedy at Corinth was for the brethren to walk in love towards one another. We properly represent God when we recognize that He doesn't need any sacrifices from us to Him. He is not watching out to see whether we eat bread and drink wine in some supposed ordinance. He shows us that it is other saints who live amongst us that need our sacrifices.

22 What! have ye not houses to eat and to drink in? or despise ye the church of God, and shame them that have not? What shall I say to you? shall I praise you in this? I praise you not.
1 Corinthians 11:22

If the saints wanted to eat at their convenience and at their own pace, they had their houses for that. This supper, which the saints were to have in their fellowship meetings was to be a feast of love. Divine love would wait for all the saints to come together before anyone descends upon the feast. The self-correction that each saint should do in the light of "this do in remembrance of me" is to share with others as a recognition of Christ's sacrifice.

On a lighter note, Paul dealt with some practical matters.

Hungry? Eat at home.

It makes sense to eat before going for a Christian service. Hungry people are more open to yielding to the flesh. When we are hungry it is harder to prioritize the love walk. A rumbling belly could hinder the love walk. Part of practical preparation for their services would have been ensuring that the family is fed before they leave for church meetings.

Thus, we see that the message within the Lord's supper is giving to others sacrificially like Christ gave Himself as our Passover. Paul later fully teaches this in 1 Corinthians 13. In 1 Corinthians 11 he showed the physical consequence of not walking in love. Our cold, hungry and destitute brethren are deprived of care and they experience the consequences of neglect in an imperfect world. For those who indulge their appetites, the excess destroys their body balance resulting in tragedy.

In any case, the answer is that the saints' greatest need is to recognize the riches of kindness and liberality.

Why the long-winded answer?

He had said, "I have fed you with milk, and not with meat" (see 1 Corinthians 3:2), which means that in 1 Corinthians 11, he couldn't speak plainly. He spoke as unto carnal and not as unto spiritual. He shows that not giving to those who lack is denying the power to lay down our lives for another. He served His body as his love to us. Therefore, we receive Christ's sacrifice as the message to live for one another by not closing our bowels. Instead, we care for one another.

When the Lord said, "this is my body broken for you", He was not drawing attention to the physical bread in His hands but to see the supply of bread in the sacrifice of Christ. That is the end of selfishness in the human heart. The lesson was not about the sacredness of bread and wine. Christ as heavenly bread is the end of selfishness.

The bread Jesus gave was Himself as God's love taught and preached to His hearers. The way to show we understand that message is to no longer be ruled by greed. We recognize that at the moment that we that believe eat Jesus as bread by receiving Christ as life, we become that bread.

5

Malachi's Prophecy

25. Then he said unto them, O fools, and slow of heart to believe all that the prophets have spoken:26. Ought not Christ to have suffered these things, and to enter into his glory? 27. And beginning at Moses and all the prophets, he expounded unto them in all the scriptures the things concerning himself.
Luke 24:25 - 27

Jesus concerned Himself with those utterances of the prophets that were to produce faith in their hearers. Such utterances were concerning Him. The word translated "fools" means "lacking in proper understanding." These disciples did not properly understand all that the prophets had said, which should have produced faith. Jesus explained all those faith-giving utterances of the prophets. He did not explain everything the prophets said. The prophets spoke about many other things which did not give faith. He expounded only those things that they said regarding the sufferings of Christ and His entering into His glory.

44. And he said unto them, These are the words which I spake unto you, while I was yet with you, that all things must be fulfilled, which were written in the law of Moses, and in the prophets, and in the psalms, concerning me. 45. Then opened he their understanding, that they might understand the scriptures, 46. And said unto them, Thus it is written, and thus it behoved Christ to suffer, and to rise from the dead the third day:
Luke 24:44 – 46

Jesus explained those aspects of the law of Moses, the prophets, and the psalms that give faith. The word "fulfilled" in "all things must be fulfilled" refers to discharging an obligation or duty. Those portions of the prophets' utterances that give faith are an assignment that Jesus was obligated to perform. Jesus has performed all those prophecies, since the portions that gives faith are concern Him. Jesus is the message of Moses, the prophets, and the psalms. A man that understands all other aspects of scripture but doesn't understand those utterances that give faith, doesn't understand the scriptures at all – the scriptures are closed to him and he needs his understanding opened.

The word translated "opened" carries the idea of opening for the first time. This means that lacking Jesus' explanation of those faith-giving prophecies of the scriptures, they had not understood the scriptures. Simply put, Christ is the understanding of the Holy scriptures. Jesus' bias in explaining scriptures was to show that the sufferings of the Christ and the glory to follow are the "all things" of the scripture of the prophets. A man is ready to understand scriptures when he can see that the bible is a closed book until explained in the light of the redemption that is in Christ.

He only explained "Moses and all the prophets" and gave them importance in relation to how those prophecies foretold what He would accomplish in death and resurrection. He showed that He is the content of the promises of scriptures.

The disciples had a long-standing challenge of not believing the death and resurrection:

21. From that time forth began Jesus to shew unto his disciples, how that he must go unto Jerusalem, and suffer many things of the elders and chief priests and scribes, and be killed, and be raised again the third day. 22. Then Peter took him, and began to rebuke him, saying, Be it far from thee, Lord: this shall not be unto thee

Matthew 16:21 - 22

Before His death, Jesus had started to show from scriptures the particulars of His death and resurrection on the third day. His disciples showed their ignorance of scriptures by rejecting Jesus' explanation of the faith-giving utterances of the holy scriptures. They had been in unbelief.

45. Then opened he their understanding, that they might understand the scriptures, 46. And said unto them, Thus it is written, and thus it behoved Christ to suffer, and to rise from the dead the third day: 47. And that repentance and remission of sins should be preached in his name among all nations, beginning at Jerusalem. 48. And ye are witnesses of these things.
Luke 24:45 - 48

Their eyes opened the first time that they saw Christ as the one whose obligation it was to fulfil the utterance of the prophets. Their eyes had been previously closed by their failure to see Christ as central to what is written in scriptures. Jesus used His explanation of Christ as the subject matter of the prophecies to open their understanding. The Lord Jesus showed that the thread that holds all the prophecies of scripture together is that "it behoved Christ to suffer, and to rise from the dead the third day". Understanding the bible as a book about Christ, a book of redemption is the bias that opens up the bible to make it a brand-new book.

The disciples of Jesus only began to understand Jesus' teaching after His resurrection. It was this teaching that He gave after His resurrection that unlocked all else that He had said to them during His three and half years with them.

More importantly, Jesus' bias in bible study was to focus on those faith-giving prophecies of the prophets that spoke about Christ's suffering and entering into His glory. He began His study at Moses and traced this throughout the writings of the prophets until He had covered all scripture – this is Genesis to Malachi.

Peter approached the scriptures this way too:

9. Receiving the end of your faith, even the salvation of your souls. 10. Of which salvation the prophets have enquired and searched diligently, who prophesied of the grace that should come unto you: 11. Searching what, or what manner of time the Spirit of Christ which was in them did signify, when it

testified beforehand the sufferings of Christ, and the glory that should follow.
1 Peter 1:9 – 11

The faith-giving prophecies of the prophets were about God's salvation plan, which was the grace to come. Through those prophecies, God was signifying "the sufferings of Christ, and the glory that should follow."

We see this in Paul too:

22. Having therefore obtained help of God, I continue unto this day, witnessing both to small and great, saying none other things than those which the prophets and Moses did say should come:
23. That Christ should suffer, and that he should be the first that should rise from the dead, and should shew light unto the people, and to the Gentiles.
Acts 26:22 - 23

Paul said that when he preached "that Christ should suffer, and that he should be the first that should rise from the dead" he preached "none other things than those which the prophets and Moses did say should come."

Peter and Paul agreed with Jesus that Genesis to Malachi converge on Christ who God has raised from the dead.

The message of the prophets is the sufferings of Christ and the glory to follow. Thus, when we read the writings of the prophets we should follow Jesus' biased reading by watching out for the sufferings of Christ and the glories that should follow. If we cannot find the truths of His suffering and His resurrection, we re-examine our reading or conclude that the prophet is not major.

Jesus, the Messenger of the covenant

Malachi was a prophet. We will approach his prophecy with this Christ-bias. We understand the scriptures by understanding how Jesus has taught it.

1. Behold, I will send my messenger, and he shall prepare the way before me: and the Lord, whom ye seek, shall suddenly come to his temple, even the messenger of the covenant, whom ye delight in: behold, he shall come, saith the LORD of hosts.
Malachi 3:1

Two messengers are spoken of – the messenger to prepare the way. This refers to another prophet who immediately precedes the Lord to point Him out. The message of this prophet is that the people should believe on the one coming after Him (see Acts 19:4). This is John who Jesus called the greatest prophet (see Luke 7:28). John does very well what every other prophet was to do – he prophesied of the coming Redeemer. John was the greatest because he was the one who could point Jesus out. The other messenger is the Messenger of the covenant. Malachi identified the Messenger of the covenant as "the Lord, whom ye seek, shall suddenly come to his temple."

8. Now I say that Jesus Christ was a minister of the circumcision for the truth of God, to confirm the promises made unto the fathers:
Romans 15:8

Jesus Christ was a minister of the circumcision. He was the confirmation or surety of those promises that God had made unto the fathers.

Malachi's messenger of the covenant is the Lord Jesus, while the messenger that shall "prepare the way before me" is John the Baptist whose ministry prepared the way for Jesus by telling people to believe Him.

He has purified the priesthood

2. But who may abide the day of his coming? and who shall stand when he appeareth? for he is like a refiner's fire, and like fullers' soap: 3. And he shall sit as a refiner and purifier of silver: and he shall purify the sons of Levi, and purge them as gold and silver, that they may offer unto the LORD an offering in righteousness.
Malachi 3:2 - 3

Jesus' refiner's fire, fullers' soap and purging refer to His coming as the cleansing from sin by His resurrection.

The answer to the question, "who shall stand when he appeareth?" is that none shall stand.

The sons of Levi are the Aaron's priesthood who ministered under the shadow. In Hebrews the Lord brings an end to that priesthood by fulfilling what they were signifying. He also brings an end to their earthly tabernacle by showing that God never had any interest in buildings built by human hands (see Acts 7:47-49). He shows that the people purified are the building or house of God that He dwells in (see Ephesians 2:22, Hebrews 3:6). He sits (and remains seated) at the right hand of majesty having offered sacrifices for sins once and for all.

Malachi had prophesied that this messenger of the covenant will come cleaning with power. This is Jesus' work as the One who cleanses from sin.

14. For by one offering he hath perfected for ever them that are sanctified.
Hebrews 10:14

He has purged our sins once and forever. We are permanently sanctified. All that are in Christ are sanctified through the one offering of the body of Jesus Christ. It is once (this shows the first time was more than enough). "It is once" means it is not repeated (the sons of Levi used to repeat their sacrifices). It is once and it is forever. This is so potent and thorough that it cannot conceivably be improved upon by any – not even God Himself. It is once and for all. The reason why the old sacrifices offered by the old priesthood could never save was not on account of the magnitude of the sins of men. It was because the sacrifices of that priesthood were completely weak and powerless. A powerless sacrifice means a powerless priesthood. The priests are as complete as the sacrifice of that priesthood. "Where remission of these is, there is no more offering for sin" (see Hebrews 10:18).

The Lord Jesus has purified the priesthood by becoming the High Priest. He has purified the sacrificial system by removing our dark assumptions about the sacrificial system. He has abolished the old temple, priesthood, sacrificial system and ordinances, which were impotent to deal with sin. Although, on the day of atonement, Aaron's priesthood shows God as punisher, in Christ, God acts apart from Aaron's priesthood, sets aside its faulty imagery and shows that He has never desired sacrifice (see Isaiah 1:11-14, Psalm 40:6, Hebrews 10:5-8). Death is not God's judgment. It is sin's penalty (see Romans 6:23). The act of sacrificing carries with it the illusion that sacrifice is for God. the Messenger of the covenant shows that God is not the beneficiary of sacrifice. Instead He takes our place and offers on our behalf.

We are made priests by His resurrection (see 1 Peter 2:5,9). They shall "offer unto the LORD an offering in righteousness" means that we take our example from the right actions of the Messenger of the covenant by recognizing that God has not desired sacrifices for Himself. Rather than offer Him sacrifices, we fulfil His pleasure by recognizing that our love-walk meets the needs of other men who live amongst us. They are the ones that need our sacrifices.

Just as Malachi had prophesied, none stands – the old priesthood is sacked, all that believe have obtained mercy and are made priests seated in Him (see Ephesians 2:6).

Who is He against in Malachi 3:5?

5. And I will come near to you to judgment; and I will be a swift witness against the sorcerers, and against the adulterers, and against false swearers, and against those that oppress the hireling in his wages, the widow, and the fatherless, and that turn aside the stranger from his right, and fear not me, saith the LORD of hosts.

Malachi 3:5

These sorcerers are those who resist the gospel, speak evil of it, and hide the truth of salvation from the people they minister to. Jesus comes as the faithful witness "that loved us, and washed us from our sins in His own blood" (see Revelation 1:5). His washing us from our sins is His witness against unbelief. This is the judgment of unbelief.

22. Thou shalt truly tithe all the increase of thy seed, that the field bringeth forth year by year. 23. And thou shalt eat before the LORD thy God, in the place which he shall choose to place his name there, the tithe of thy corn, of thy wine, and of thine oil, and the firstlings of thy herds and of thy flocks; that thou mayest learn to fear the LORD thy God always.
Deuteronomy 14:22 - 23

28. At the end of three years thou shalt bring forth all the tithe of thine increase the same year, and shalt lay it up within thy gates:
29. And the Levite, (because he hath no part nor inheritance with thee,) and the stranger, and the fatherless, and the widow, which are within thy gates, shall come, and shall eat and be satisfied; that the LORD thy God may bless thee in all the work of thine hand which thou doest.
Deuteronomy 14:28 – 29

Moses taught the people that in the third year, all were to eat the tithe so that "thou mayest learn to fear the LORD thy God always." That expression "The fear of the LORD" is a figure of speech.

The psalmist said, "The LORD takes pleasure in those who fear him, in those who hope in his unfailing steadfast love" (see Psalm 147:11). Thus, to "fear the Lord" means to hope "in His unfailing steadfast love." The fear of the Lord is the security of the believer.

Isaiah's prophecy of Jesus, "and shall make him of quick understanding in the fear of the LORD" (see Isaiah 11:3). "The fear of the LORD" does not mean that the Lord Jesus was afraid of the Father or scared of Him, it means that the Lord Jesus was quick to teach His understanding of God's unfailing steadfast love.

In Acts, Luke described the effect of Paul's ministry as, "then had the churches rest throughout all Judaea and Galilee and Samaria, and were edified; and walking in the fear of the Lord, and in the comfort of the Holy Ghost, were multiplied" (see Acts 9:31). "The fear of the Lord" is associated with rest for those that believe. To fear the Lord does not mean to shake before Him like one who has seen a rattle snake.

The fear of the Lord means not to be afraid of God. It is hope in the salvation of God, which is His unfailing love in Christ. Thus, when Moses taught the eating of the tithe "so that thou mayest learn to fear the LORD thy God always", he was teaching the people to hope in the salvation of God – His unfailing steadfast love. Moses reason for teaching the eating of the tithe was to communicate the truth of God's provision of salvation. Thus, under the shadow, the tithe was a provision for the Levites, the stranger, the fatherless, and the widow – it was for all who had no inheritance or had lost their inheritance. Salvation would be the inheritance of the man who believes.

7. Even from the days of your fathers ye are gone away from mine ordinances, and have not kept them. Return unto me, and I will return unto you, saith the LORD of hosts. But ye said, Wherein shall we return? 8. Will a man rob God? Yet ye have robbed me. But ye say, Wherein have we robbed thee? In tithes and offerings.
Malachi 3:7 - 8

We know Malachi is addressing the priests because he had said, "And now, O ye priests, this commandment is for you" (see Malachi 2:1).

They had robbed God in not providing "meat" or the tithe to be eaten as Moses had instructed them to do. The stranger, the fatherless, and the widow (we'll classify all these as the poor) were denied the blessing of eating of the tithe "so that thou mayest learn to fear the LORD thy God always."

The stranger, the fatherless, and the widow represent those without inheritance rights to fend for themselves. The Levites and Priests could not provide. They had gone away from Deuteronomy 14.

The Levitical Priesthood had abandoned Moses' teaching of the eating of the tithe as a mechanism for communicating the truth of God's provision of salvation. In so doing they had robbed God of what God wanted to do – save men by giving them the inheritance of His unfailing love. God's plan was for men to turn from the blindness of unbelief so they could receive the inheritance of the forgiveness of sins (see Acts 26:18).

There would be meat in "My house"

What would be the consequence when the Levites received the correction from the Messenger of the covenant?

There would be meat in "My house."

Malachi had already said, "The Lord, whom ye seek, shall suddenly come to his temple" (see Malachi 3:1). His message had not changed. The Lord in "His Temple" is "meat in my house."

Stephen clarifies that Malachi's reference to "My house" or "His Temple" cannot refer to the structure built by Solomon. He said, "Solomon built him an house. Howbeit the most High dwelleth not in temples made with hands; as saith the prophet" (see Acts 7:47 - 48). Therefore, the prophets knew that "My house" was other than the temple in Jerusalem. God had promised David that He would build David a temple. This is the tabernacle of David - the new creation as God's temple. "My house" refers to the people that God would redeem.

Malachi's "My house" would be a reference to the widow, orphan, poor and stranger who had been deprived of eating of the tithe "so that thou mayest learn to fear the LORD thy God always." Malachi admits that the priests had failed to see to it that there was meat in the house.

Malachi's curse refers to the absence of meat in "My house." This corresponds to the lack of supply of tithe to be eaten "so that thou mayest learn to fear the LORD thy God always." The curse is failing to receive the inheritance of God's unfailing love.

Malachi's prophecy is that God Himself will pour out the blessing (see Malachi 3:10). The blessing would be God's direct action by the Messenger of the covenant, who as a priest would be the answer to the impotence of the Levitical priesthood. Malachi prophesied that God would "pour you out a blessing, that there shall not be room enough to receive it" (see Malachi 3:10). This is God emptying out the goodness and mercy in His heart until the people are overwhelmed with His unfailing steadfast love. This new priest would bring the true tithe (the blessing) to the storehouse (not a place, but a people - the widow, orphan, and stranger, which refers to the poor). This priest brings the blessing to those who did not have the blessing. In this way, all the tithe will come into the storehouse so that there is meat in "My house." Man would live in the fulfilment of God's unfailing steadfast love, which Moses used the eating of the tithe to teach.

Malachi's prophecy is strong consolation that the Messenger of the covenant would fulfil the tithe ordinance for the tithe ordinance cannot be fulfilled by human power but by God Himself.

Who is bringing the tithe?

10. Bring ye all the tithes into the storehouse, that there may be meat in mine house, and prove me now herewith, saith the LORD of hosts, if I will not open you the windows of heaven, and pour you out a blessing, that there shall not be room enough to receive it.

Malachi 3:10

The word translated "ye" in the King James version is a Hebrew word that occurs over 7000 times but has only been translated about 100 times. The translators hardly translate this word that has been translated "ye" because they don't really know its meaning.

Since the word "ye" is hardly translated, an alternate and clearer reading of "bring ye all the tithes into the storehouse" is "bring all the tithes into the storehouse."

The big question: Who is bringing the tithe?

These are the words of prophet Malachi. They are faith-giving words. It is not something we perform. We are to believe the words of the prophets (see Romans 10:16, Acts 26:27, Luke 24:25).

This agrees with what Jesus told His disciples, "all things must be fulfilled, which were written in the law of Moses, and in the prophets, and in the psalms, concerning me" (see Luke 24:44). The word translated "fulfil" speaks of an obligation to be discharged. Jesus wants us to see Him as the one obligated to perform those portions of the prophets' utterances that give faith – they are the documentation of His assignment.

Jesus would say that "bring ye all the tithes into the storehouse" is concerning Him. It is a task for Him to discharge!

The psalmist gives us tremendous insight:

6 Sacrifice and offering thou didst not desire; mine ears hast thou opened: burnt offering and sin offering hast thou not required. 7 Then said I, Lo, I come: in the volume of the book it is written of me, 8 I delight to do thy will, O my God: yea, thy law is within my heart.
Psalm 40:6-8

The writer of Hebrews says the person in psalm 40 is Jesus (see Hebrews 10:5-7).

The word translated "volume" in "in the volume of the book" is a Hebrew word meaning the heading or title of the book. Jesus saw that the requirements of the scriptures were written of, and to Jesus and not to anyone else.

Jesus would read "bring ye all the tithes into the storehouse" and He'll see the title of that demand as addressed to Himself. To meet His obligations, God manifested in the flesh to fulfil the requirements of Malachi and the prophets.

Through understanding the scriptures, Jesus' ears were opened to see that the Father had no pleasure in sacrifice.

Jesus declaration that the volume was about Him, shows that the requirements within the holy scriptures are addressed to Him as a description of what Jesus was to do. The Law wasn't written to give us life by our compliance. The demands were a teaching of what Jesus was to do and not what we were to do. "Bring ye, the tithe, into the storehouse" is Malachi speaking to Jesus about His sacrifice.

Here is a play on words:

The "ye" in "Bring ye", is a Hebrew word made up of Aleph (the first letter of the Hebrew alphabet) and Tav (the last letter of the Hebrew alphabet), which corresponds to the Greek Alpha and Omega.

We hear Malachi say to Jesus, "bring the first and last, the tithe, into the storehouse."

In Isaiah, Jesus says, "I am the first, and I am the last" (see Isaiah 44:6).

John also shows us Jesus' response; "I am Alpha and Omega, the beginning and the ending, saith the Lord" (see Revelation 1:8).

Malachi wasn't telling the people to "bring ye all the tithes into the storehouse." He was prophesying about Christ. He was speaking to Jesus about what He would accomplish. In Malachi's words, we see God's performance.

The Brown Driver Briggs Hebrew Lexicon says that the word "ye" comes from another root word that could be severally translated as a miraculous sign, token, proof, a signal, a monument or even an omen.

An omen is the sign of a future event. Thus, Malachi wasn't prophesying of things to happen in that day but of things to come. The event that Malachi prophesied about was future to the day of Malachi.

What would be the fulfilment?

Malachi's words were, "prove me no herewith, saith the LORD of hosts, if I will not open you the windows of heaven, and pour you out a blessing." The fulfilment will be God's action of opening the windows of heaven. He pours out a blessing.

The point is that we do not give God the tithe. He gives the tithe as His gift to us. In believing the prophets, we receive the tithe from God who has freely given it to us in Christ.

Melchizedek's blessing of Abraham

The writer of Hebrews gives great insight into God's blessing by informing us of Melchizedek's blessing of Abraham:

For this Melchizedek, king of Salem, priest of the most high God, who met Abraham returning from the slaughter of the kings, and blessed him;
Hebrews 7:1

The writer of Hebrews speaks of Melchizedek, who as priest of the most high God, blessed Abraham.

The scripture teaches that High Priests are taken from among men to offer "both gifts and sacrifices for sins" (see Hebrews 5:1).

This means that the wealth, blessing or favour that flows from a High Priest is blessing in relation to sins being dealt with. The biblical ministry of High Priests is not given in relation to increasing financial or material. It settles the sin problem.

The fact of the non-material nature of this blessing is obvious since Moses confirms that when Abram met Melchizedek, Abram was already very rich in cattle, in silver, and in gold (see Genesis 13:2). Abram, who was already rich in cattle, in silver, and in gold was still in need of being blessed by Melchizedek. This means that Melchizedek's blessing of Abraham is not material riches. Abram did not need Melchizedek for more gold, he needed the blessing of a priest, which is assurance that his sins will be dealt with.

David knew and preached this blessedness. He spoke of "the blessedness of the man, unto whom God imputeth righteousness without works" (see Romans 4: 6).

Again, what is this blessing?

To bless means to speak well. As a priest of the most high God, Melchizedec's blessing of Abraham would mean that Melchizedec spoke well of Abram concerning how God would deal with Abram's sins. This means Melchizedec repeated to Abram God's promise to bless him, which God had spoken in Genesis 12:3.

Abraham's blessing

These are the wordings of Abraham's blessing:

3 and I will bless them that bless thee, and curse him that curseth thee: and in thee shall all families of the earth be blessed.
Genesis 12:3

God who promised the blessing to Abram is the only one that gives the blessing of Abraham.

And the scripture, foreseeing that God would justify the heathen through faith, preached before the gospel unto Abraham, saying, In thee shall all nations be blessed.
Galatians 3:8

Paul explains "Abraham's blessing" as God's blessing of justifying the heathen through faith.

Peter explained Abraham's blessing:

25. Ye are the children of the prophets, and of the covenant which God made with our fathers, saying unto Abraham, And in thy seed shall all the kindreds of the earth be blessed. 26. Unto you first God, having raised up his Son Jesus, sent him to bless you, in turning away every one of you from his iniquities.
Acts 3:26

God's promise to bless all the kindreds of the earth is God's justification of the heathen through faith by the resurrection of Christ. By raising Jesus from the dead, God has opened to us the windows of heaven and poured us out a blessing – It is the blessing of turning us away from our iniquities! The blessing is the sacrifice of His son for sins and by this resurrection, the sinner is justified.

Jesus, in His sacrifice, is the windows of heaven opened and poured out on the believing one.

Paul explained the blessing of Abraham further:

13. Christ hath redeemed us from the curse of the law, being made a curse for us: for it is written, Cursed is every one that hangeth on a tree: 14. That the blessing of Abraham might come on the Gentiles through Jesus Christ; that we might receive the promise of the Spirit through faith.
Galatians 3: 13 – 14

The curse refers to the fact that the blessing of Abraham had not come.

The blessing of Abraham is specifically the promise of the Spirit through faith.

Therefore, what the people did not have was the promise of the Spirit through faith. There was no meat in "My house."

God has poured out Abraham's blessing that He promised in Malachi. Jesus is the tithe that has brought the blessing into the storehouse.

What is Abraham's blessing?

We observe that all through the Epistles, the blessing of Abraham or the promise is always spoken of in the singular.

It is the reception of the promise of the Spirit through faith. Thus, Melchizedek blessed Abram by repeating to him the ancient promise of God's spirit indwelling man thus making man the temple of God.

The overwhelming evidence of explanation in the Epistles is that Abraham's blessing, which is the blessing God has poured out in fulfilment of Malachi's prophecy was not material riches but the true riches of a recreated spirit perfected in Christ forever. The promised blessing poured out by God in Malachi was not money but a new spirit given to man on account of Jesus' resurrection.

Abraham received the promise of Christ's death burial and resurrection in a figure (see Hebrews 11:19). Although Abraham looked forward to receiving this spirit, he never obtained the fulfilment of it in his lifetime. "These all, having obtained a good report through faith, received not the promise" (see Hebrews 11: 39).

Peter's words again:

Unto you first God, having raised up his Son Jesus, sent him to bless you, in turning away every one of you from his iniquities.
Acts 3: 26

The promise has been fulfilled. That spirit which Abraham and ancient saints never received has now been given through the resurrection of Jesus.

Thus, the gospel that Paul preached to the Galatians was that the blessing of Abraham has come on the Gentiles through Jesus Christ (see Galatians 3:14). The windows of heaven have been opened. We have received the promise of the spirit through faith and this spirit makes us sons (see Galatians 3:14, 4:6-7). We have been blessed with sonship in that we have received the spirit.

Moses and the eating of the tithe

23. And thou shalt eat before the LORD thy God, in the place which he shall choose to place his name there, the tithe of thy corn, of thy wine, and of thine oil, and the firstlings of thy herds and of thy flocks; that thou mayest learn to fear the LORD thy God always.

Deuteronomy 14:23

All through Deuteronomy 14, tithe is not a payment to the priest but something eaten. The corn, wine, oil, and firstling are the tithe, which point to Christ as food. The tithe belonged to God. God then gave His property to the people to eat. The lesson within the tithe is that we are to receive the One which God has given and to eat in order to find life in Him.

Moses did not use great plainness of speech (see 2 Corinthians 3:12-13). Removing Moses' heavy symbols, Moses taught, "Except you eat the tithe, you will not know the fear of God. Jesus is the tithe you eat to receive God's salvation or joy." Moses taught God's supply of joy by teaching the eating of the tithe.

Jesus clarifies Moses' record of the truth contained within the Manna.

Jesus said this in John:

55. For my flesh is meat indeed, and my blood is drink indeed. 56. He that eateth my flesh, and drinketh my blood, dwelleth in me, and I in him.
John 6:55 - 56

Jesus had been teaching that "the work of God" is "that ye believe on him whom he hath sent" (v29). He was teaching the people to believe on Him as the true Manna that God gives from heaven. He shows that believing is the eating of the heavenly Manna (v35). Jesus affirmed that He is the fulfilment of the manna as the bread of life or life-giving bread (v48).

Jesus says, "my flesh is meat indeed."

We eat Jesus' "flesh and blood" by receiving His words and not by biting His skin. He said, "the words that I speak unto you, they are spirit, and they are life" (see John 6:63). It is in the words of the gospel that Jesus' "flesh and blood" are given. The man that receives the gospel has eaten Jesus as the meat. This is how meat comes into God's house.

Jesus is the fulfilment of what the manna pointed to. He is the manna that fell from heaven. You eat Jesus as tithe by believing. Therefore, the curse is abiding in unbelief trying to obtain life by performance. That curse is broken in the supply of Christ who was made sin for us so that the believing ones are made the righteousness of God.

Lessons from Moses' manna

15. And when the children of Israel saw it, they said one to another, It is manna: for they wist not what it was. And Moses said unto them, This is the bread which the LORD hath given you to eat. 16. This is the thing which the LORD hath commanded, Gather of it every man according to his eating, an omer for every man, according to the number of your persons; take ye every man for them which are in his tents. 17. And the children of Israel did so, and gathered, some more, some less. 18. And when they did mete it with an omer, he that gathered much had nothing over, and he that gathered little had no lack; they gathered every man according to his eating.
Exodus 16:15 - 18

Jesus clarified Moses' words, "This is the bread which the LORD hath given you to eat." He said, "Moses gave you not that bread from heaven; but my Father giveth you the true bread from heaven" (see John 6: 32). Moses wasn't referring to the food that they were looking at. Moses was teaching them of Christ who is the true Manna from God.

How much manna could each person have? It was as much as each person liked.

Interestingly, although "they gathered each man according to his eating", when measured, each man had exactly one omer of manna! No one needed more than one omer. Furthermore, Moses tells us that this Omer is a tithe of an ephah (v36). Thus, the portion of the manna for each person is a tithe.

The Hebrew word translated "Omer" is from a primitive root (amar) that means "to heap; figuratively to chastise (as if piling blows); specifically, to gather grain." Figuratively, the Manna is the tithe, which would suffer by receiving blows and chastisement so as to be eaten. This is the gospel in parable form, for the tithe on whom the blows fell was Christ. Jesus is not only the manna and the tithe, He is the lamb, as well as the first fruit. Jesus as the tithe means that He fulfilled what the tithe stood for. He is the tithe who said, "Take, eat: this is my body, which is broken for you: this do in remembrance of me" (see 1 Corinthians 11:24). The lesson in the manna is that no one brought Manna (which is a tithe) to God. Manna represents God's provision of Jesus as the life-giving bread, which we eat.

The tithe is not what we owe God but what He has freely given us.

While Israel walked in the wilderness, they had no inheritance. The provision to be eaten back then was the manna. Manna is the food to give life to the world. The manna and the tithe both teach of Christ.

By one sacrifice

The writer of Hebrews shows that Jesus the tithe is the one-time sacrifice. The writer of Hebrews says, "For by one offering he hath perfected for ever them that are sanctified" (see Hebrews 10:12,14). He is not eaten daily. He was provided once in order that the believing one might eat Him once, for He had prophesied, "I am the bread of life: he that cometh to me shall never hunger; and he that believeth on me shall never thirst (see John 6:35).

Once is all it takes because once is enough. He is that potent. God has exceeded requirements in giving Jesus as the tithe. Malachi's prophecy has been fulfilled, "there shall not be room enough to receive it" (see Malachi 3:10). The tithe has been so totally once-for-all fulfilled in Christ Jesus that there is no other way of keeping it.

When we give, we are not trying to get Malachi's blessing. Malachi's blessing, Abraham's blessing, Melchizedek's blessing is one and the same thing. It is the teaching that Jesus is the giver of the spirit as proof that we have been cleansed from all our sins once and for all.

Now that we have eaten Jesus as the tithe, we also live for others in remembrance of Him. The same Spirit by which Christ gave Himself for others has been reproduced in us, so I give for God is the Father of my giving. I learn the truth of the gospel and I give to others to express the riches of liberality and to exercise contentment which is my freedom from covetousness.

6

Let Him Give

Luke gives us insight into how the Lord Jesus executed His post-resurrection teaching ministry.

Then opened he their understanding, that they might understand the scriptures,
Luke 24:45

The Greek word translated "opened" in "then opened he their understanding" is opening for the first time. It is the opening of that which had never been opened before.

Although these men could quote those prophecies as well as Jesus, their eyes had been closed to the truth of what they quoted. Jesus did not merely quote. Jesus distinguished Himself in explaining scriptures and not in quoting. They had been quoting the scriptures but lacking the explanation that would help them see its message. Jesus' explanation removed their blindness to the message of the scriptures. We must not confuse profuse quoting of scriptures with understanding its message. The New Testament minister distinguishes himself by explaining rather than merely quoting profusely.

The word "understanding" in "He opened their understanding" refers to their mind, perspectives or slant, whereas the word "understand" in "that they might understand" is not referring to the mind. It means the bringing or joining together of things in the mind. The Lord Jesus brought together the various prophecies in the law of Moses, the prophets, and the psalms that give faith and His explanation showed that the thread that holds all those faith-giving prophecies together is that "it behoved Christ to suffer, and to rise from the dead the third day". He used the correct explanation of scriptures to open the understanding of His disciples to see that He was the truth of the holy scriptures concerning sacrifice for sins. As a result of understanding, these disciples would have stopped presenting bulls and rams as sacrifice for sins. Furthermore, as they grow in their grasp of understanding Christ as the sacrifice of scriptures, they'll come to see their identification with Him. In acknowledging that identification, they yield to Him living His life as a sacrifice through them for others.

Although we are tempted to treat it as reference material, the Bible is not designed for quoting. It is to be explained so as to open the eyes and heart of the reader. A careful reading of the temptation of Jesus shows that whereas the devil merely quoted to communicate his stance, Jesus used scriptures to explain other scriptures (see Luke 4:3-13). Jesus shows that when we use scriptures correctly, the devil flees.

Acknowledging of every good thing

6. That the communication of thy faith may become effectual by the acknowledging of every good thing which is in you in Christ Jesus.
Philemon 1:6

The word translated "communication" here is usually translated fellowship. Fellowship means the supply (and reception of that which is supplied). In this case it is the supply of faith. Paul is really praying that Philemon would share to others that which God had shared to him in Christ. God's riches in His saint is a capacity to share that is given to the saint in Christ. The saint is to acknowledge this.

The word translated "acknowledging" here means precise knowledge. This Greek word means to understand clearly, thoroughly and fully.

The saint is to have a precise understanding of God's riches in Christ, which the saint then acknowledges to be true of him or her. The supply of faith improves with precise knowledge about God's seed in us. When we clearly understand God's riches as seen in His Son, we gain the knowledge of the facts of the riches He has given us in the New Birth. It is by acknowledgment of the sacrifice of Christ that we become fruitful in that knowledge for it defines who we are.

The Amplified Bible states it this way, "I pray that the sharing of your faith may become effective and powerful because of your accurate knowledge of every good thing which is ours in Christ".

Christ Jesus is God's supply of faith to all. Thus, the saint doesn't need to get faith. Instead, the faith is supplied as the message and the saint is to study the Word so as to know in minute detail the faith already made available in Christ. We acknowledge what has been supplied in Christ because the knowledge of Christ is the working definition of what the believer is.

This fact that the fellowship of faith becomes more effectual with precise explanation is the reason why we use teaching to clarify the particulars about God's riches in the man who is born again.

14 Of these things put them in remembrance, charging them before the Lord that they strive not about words to no profit, but to the subverting of the hearers.
2 Timothy 2:14

Paul warns Timothy to remind the ministers under him not to be unskillful or illiterate when it comes to the truths of redemption. Those who are illiterate end up preaching sermons that subvert the saints who hear them – it ruins the confidence of the saints in what the Lord has done. This subverting of saints does not happen in the red-light district, in pubs or beer parlors. Subversion is enforced by what people hear preached from the pulpit when saints gather together. These teachings veil the saints from acknowledging the riches of God's grace in them.

How would the ministers recover from peddling subversion?

15 Study to shew thyself approved unto God, a workman that needeth not to be ashamed, rightly dividing the word of truth.
2 Timothy 2:15

The word translated "study" means to be an understudy. It means that we do our best in the ministry of the word. "Rightly dividing" means to cut through correctly, it means to handle well, skillfully or correctly. Teachers and preachers of the gospels are to pay attention to the Word and the words that have been used to convey Bible truth correctly. We believe its content within the context that it has been used and correctly teach its truth with accuracy and skill.

Timothy was to distinguish himself from those who peddle wrong doctrine because they handle God's word without skill or accuracy. We distinguish ourselves by seeing to it that through study we accurately handle the word of truth.

Paul is not saying that study is what makes God approve the minister. The minister is approved by God in Christ. The problem is not "approved of God", the problem at hand is ministers preaching subversion to saints. The minister repents of subversion by studying and teaching in the light of that understanding that the Lord Jesus conveyed when He brought together the various prophecies in the law of Moses, the prophets, and the psalms.

Here is the Passion translation:

Always be eager to present yourself before God as a perfect and mature minister, without shame, as one who correctly explains the Word of Truth
2 Timothy 2:15 (TPT)

In the margin of The Passion Translation, the translators show that an alternate Aramaic translation of "Study to shew thyself" is "Don't become frustrated." The Greek word is spoudazo, an aorist imperative verb that could be translated, "Hurry and keep on hurrying," or "Consider it a serious matter and keep on considering it something serious to present yourself before God."

Paul does not want Timothy to be a part of the systematic miseducation that makes saints become dull to the riches of kindness and liberality which has been received by each saint in the New Birth.

The Lord knoweth them that are His

17. And their word will eat as doth a canker: of whom is Hymenaeus and Philetus; 18. Who concerning the truth have erred, saying that the resurrection is past already; and overthrow the faith of some. 19. Nevertheless the foundation of God standeth sure, having this seal, The Lord knoweth them that are his. And, Let every one that nameth the name of Christ depart from iniquity.
2 Timothy 2:17 - 19

"Their word will eat as doth a canker" refers to the spoken ministry of Hymenaeus and Philetus, who had erred "saying". Thus, Hymenaeus and Philetus are examples of ministers who have failed to consider the skilful and accurate presentation of truth as a serious matter.

The foundation of God that stands sure or firm is a reference to the truth of the resurrection, which is the firm foundation that Hymenaeus and Philetus had attempted to shift by their teaching.

Since the term "the foundation of God" is a reference to the truth of resurrection, the "them" in "the Lord knoweth them that are His" is not referring to the ministers but to the things that they taught. The truth of resurrection is God's foundation. "Them that are His" means the explanations called the doctrine of Christ. We are to teach the scriptures the way Jesus has taught it. The minister is to teach those truths that reveal God's exceeding great power as clearly seen in the resurrection of Jesus. The "them that are His" are those explanations He has given to us in the Epistles.

"The name of the Lord" refers to the Lord's reputation or what the Lord is known for, which is a figure of speech for His reputation. The gospel is the name of the Lord because it is the document of God's actions. Therefore, "to name the name of the Lord" means to preach that Christ has fulfilled His obligations as required in the prophecies of scriptures. "All that name the name of the Lord" refers to those that teach or preach doctrine. Our teachings must not associate the Lord with that which is not His exploit or else that which denies His exploit altogether. The ministers that speak contrary to the truth of resurrection display gross ungodly behaviour.

Paul told the Corinthians, "For we write none other things unto you, than what ye read or acknowledge; and I trust ye shall acknowledge even to the end" (see 2 Corinthians 1:13). Paul meant that he couldn't say or write any other thing that differed from those foundational truths already written to the churches. If he had done so, he would have qualified as one who ministered subversion to saints. Iniquity from a minister's perspective would be taking those things that God has not given us and teaching it as doctrine, especially when those things are contrary to the revelation of God's power at work in His saints in Christ. The highest immorality is sinning against the revelation of the truth of the gospel by preaching things that are contrary to the truth of Christ as God's riches in His saints. This iniquity that Paul warned the minister to depart from is due to not considering the skillful and accurate presentation of the truths of the gospel a serious matter.

The sacrifice of praise

15 By him therefore let us offer the sacrifice of praise to God continually, that is, the fruit of our lips giving thanks to his name. 16 But to do good and to communicate forget not: for with such sacrifices God is well pleased.
Hebrews 13:15-16

The Him in "By him therefore" signifies the Lord Jesus who has purified our faulty ideas about the sacrificial system. Men are under the illusion that sacrifice is for God. Jesus has shown that God could not be the beneficiary of sacrifice for He provided the sacrifice in redemption. The riches of the sacrifice of Christ who gave Himself for our sins is that by that one sacrifice, we have been sanctified forever (see Hebrews 10:14). "Let us offer the sacrifice of praise to God" means that the sacrifice of Christ directly produces a life of sacrifice in the saint. The riches that caused Christ to give Himself sacrificially are present in the saint and enables the saint to offer the sacrifice of praise to God. The sacrifice of Christ for men and the spiritual sacrifice of the saints are the sacrifices that God is well pleased with for God supplies His suffering for our good. He laid down His life for our sins (see v12). Since the discussion is about brotherly love, we know that it is men who receive these sacrifices.

No matter what, make room in your heart to love every believer.
Hebrews 13:1 (TPT)

As an illustration of brotherly love, the writer instructs "be not forgetful to entertain strangers". The saint forgets brotherly love by shutting their bowels to the indwelling riches of God's grace, mercy and kindness already received in Christ. The praise here is our response to God's love, which shows up in our lives in that we love the brethren with the riches of God's love (see verse 3). It is this not forgetting but remembering brotherly love that the writer explains as offering "the sacrifice of praise" in verses 15 & 16.

How can the saints know they have forgotten the example of Christ's sacrifice?

5 Let your conversation be without covetousness; and be content with such things as ye have: for he hath said, I will never leave thee, nor forsake thee.
Hebrews 13:5

"I will never leave thee, nor forsake thee" is God giving continual assurance that the salvation abides. We find contentment in the riches of salvation. This is freedom from covetousness. Covetousness prioritizes the riches of this world over God's riches seen in Christ.

15 So we no longer offer up a steady stream of blood sacrifices, but through Jesus, we will offer up to God a steady stream of praise sacrifices—these are "the lambs" we offer from our lips that celebrate his name! 16 We will show mercy to the poor and not miss an opportunity to do acts of kindness for others, for these are the true sacrifices that delight God's heart.
Hebrews 13:15-16 (TPT)

Offering lambs from our lips is clearly not to be taken in a literal sense. It is a figure of speech.

The Aramaic of the text speaks of "the lambs" that we offer from our lips. The lambs we offer up to God are the true sacrifices of showing the riches of mercy to the poor. We offer the riches of kindness to men. It is by such sacrifices that we showcase how rich God's mercy is.

The term "fruit" in "fruit of our lips" does not mean that literal fruits are harvested from our lips. "Fruit" is a metaphor for result, outcome or product.

Just as the lips or mouth reveal the abundance of the heart (see Matthew 12:34), our lips in "fruit of our lips" refer to how we unveil to others the riches of God in our heart. Thus, the "fruit of lips" is the riches of liberality that God has placed in our hearts. The usage of "lips" here does not mean spoken words or singing praise songs to God when we do not feel thankful or when circumstances of life are not favorable. We are speaking with our actions. John had said "My little children, let us not love in word, neither in tongue; but in deed and in truth" (see 1 John 3:18).

Giving thanks to His name

The term "giving thanks" in "giving thanks to his name" is from a Greek word that means to say the same thing as another, to be in sync, to concede or not to deny.

"His name" refers to His reputation as one who swore, "I will never leave thee, nor forsake thee." He is famed for His salvation abides. Thus, "sacrifice of praise to God continually" is recognizing that the riches of kindness that accompany salvation are always effectual in the saint. Praise is agreeing with God by cooperating with His exceeding great power that He has invested as His riches within His spirit in us. We give thanks to His name (or testify that we are sons in deed) by doing good and communicating to others.

How do we say the same thing as God?

We are continually generous as He has given Himself permanently for us. Since that great power is in us, we don't wonder what to do, we love the brethren knowing that we have the same life of sacrifice that we have seen in Christ. There is no selfishness in the life of God, therefore we let contentment rise big in us and eliminate selfishness in thought and conduct towards others.

We deny the riches of generosity in us and confuse ourselves corrupting our giving by treating it as "investment" for ourselves. In that case, what should have been a sacrifice mirroring the example of selflessness seen in Christ becomes a commercial transaction. Don't forget to love the brethren by giving of yourself and yours to minister to the saints. This is thanksgiving. This is saying the same things that God has said in the sacrifice of Christ. This is the sacrifice of praise.

17 Obey them that have the rule over you, and submit yourselves: for they watch for your souls, as they that must give account, that they may do it with joy, and not with grief: for that is unprofitable for you.
Hebrews 13:17

The writer of Hebrews describes submission as riches that we give to those who exercise oversight – our pastors who feed us the truth of God's word.

With such sacrifices God is well pleased

But to do good and to communicate forget not: for with such sacrifices God is well pleased
Hebrews 13:16

Our giving is a sacrifice of praise that pleases God for it advertises God the way He is. He is the liberal Giver who gives without finding fault (see James 1:5). This sacrifice of praise is devoid of covetousness (see Hebrews 13:5) because we have the riches of God in us always. We are "content with such things as ye have." Therefore, our giving is not investment for ourselves, it is the sacrifice of praise – His praise. Our giving is letting brotherly love continue (see Hebrews 13:1). Giving as a means to get rich is covetousness. This sacrifice of praise must be devoid of covetousness. Giving is an end in itself. It is proof of understanding the grace of God. It is not the way to increase material riches.

The life of sacrifice is set against covetousness but it is not set against giving. Its message is that God is a lavish giver who gives without finding fault in any. The riches of God that makes Him give lavishly without finding fault is His gift already given to each saint. This is characteristic of the new man. On account of the life of God within the believer, the saint wants to give. This yearning to give is part and parcel of being born again. Even in the midst of wrong teaching and bad doctrine, God's DNA of giving, which He placed in His saints at the New Birth never goes away.

Unless the saint is properly taught about giving, the slant of this world and the exertions of the flesh means that the saint would succumb to selfishness in the area of giving. This selfishness is called covetousness.

Some people are afraid that if giving was correctly taught (devoid of covetousness), saints would give less – it is assumed that saints wouldn't have a motivation for giving since there is nothing in it for them. In reality, we find that many saints give less when they first hear the milk of the word concerning giving. However, these people did not reduce their giving because they have been taught the truth. Instead, the truth helped them to start giving at the level of their hearts' persuasion devoid of the manipulations of covetousness; their hearts had been subverted by the iniquity of bad doctrine.

When these saints finally received the truth that giving was offering up spiritual sacrifices, the milk of the word was potent enough to strip away from their heart that which they had assumed was scriptural giving but was really covetousness given many fanciful names. At this point many realize that they had been investing instead of giving. Covetousness is so deadly it causes the flesh to produce non-existent revelations in the word.

Here's Paul's admonition to Timothy:

14 But continue thou in the things which thou hast learned and hast been assured of, knowing of whom thou hast learned them;
2 Timothy 3:14

The saint is to continue in the truth of salvation as riches and develop persuasion concerning the riches of liberality. It takes a while to become persuaded about giving as an end in itself. It is by continuing in the truth that persuasions are built and steps taken to depart from the iniquity of covetousness which sees giving as the path to financial harvest of money for themselves. Covetousness is iniquity. It misquotes God and puts in His mouth that which He is not saying.

As they continue to acknowledge the reality of contentment, their minds become less receptive to covetousness and they yield more to the spirit's witness concerning giving. Persuasion concerning the riches of liberality isn't automatic, the saint has to continue in it.

2 Upon the first day of the week let every one of you lay by him in store, as God hath prospered him, that there be no gatherings when I come. 3 And when I come, whomsoever ye shall approve by your letters, them will I send to bring your liberality unto Jerusalem.
1 Corinthians 16:2-3

Paul's teaching is that whatever the occasion, we are to see to it that we express liberality.

If one came to the Corinthian church and found each of them dutifully laying aside, on the first day of the week, that which they would give to others, that newcomer is not to say, "well, I am not judged by days and months" nor is he to argue that it could also be the second day of the week or the third or maybe any day for that matter. Such a person has missed the point if his argument hinders him from expressing the riches of liberality when the opportunity presents itself. The question to be asked in the light of offering up spiritual sacrifices continually should be, "have I expressed the riches of liberality in me on this occasion?"

If you find yourself in the midst of saints who don't use the right nomenclature or worse still, who believe in covetous practices, don't let their covetousness or the fact that they are not compliant with gospel terminology stop you from giving. For example, don't say, "they only asked for those who wanted to pay tithes and since I don't believe in tithes and they gave no other option I cannot give." We do not look for reasons not to give. You assure your heart about the rightness of expressing the riches of liberality. It is covetousness that is anti-gospel, giving is not.

Whatever you do, give.

The gospel destroys covetousness by opening the eyes of the saint to contentment in Christ. Contentment is the war that the spirit declares on fleshly lusts. We discover that the saint or elder that receives the explanation of God's riches in the Epistles stops having "leadings" and "seeing visions from God" that promote covetousness. The gospel aligns our motives with that of the Lord. The knowledge of Christ as God's supply to us can never be to encourage the saint to abandon giving or to give less. The rightly-divided word awakens the saint to express the riches of kindness and liberality as our family characteristics in God.

7

Some Observations

There are lessons and observations concerning the fact of the generosity of the saints in Acts and in the Epistles.

5. And this they did, not as we hoped, but first gave their own selves to the Lord, and unto us by the will of God.
2 Corinthians 8:5

This is Paul's explanation of the revelation of God's grace which had inspired the Macedonians' giving. Notice Paul's topmost priority was not how much the Macedonians gave to other men but how they first gave themselves to the Lord – this means the heart established in grace prioritises staying sensitive to perceiving God's leading. Giving based on the revelation of grace is giving to others as an overflow of giving oneself to the Lord.

Here's what Paul had taught the Corinthians earlier

Now concerning the collection for the saints, as I have given order to the churches of Galatia, even so do ye. 2 Upon the first day of the week let every one of you lay by him in store, as God hath prospered him, that there be no gatherings when I come.
1 Corinthians 16:1-2

Paul's instruction "let every one of you", which he gave to the Corinthians anticipates that every believer would practice regular giving, for it is "upon the first day of the week." "Upon the first day of the week" refers to their fellowship times as the local assembly. He said, "that there be no gatherings when I come", thus he favours saints giving in a continuous steady stream over and above giving large gifts once in a while. The "riches" of goodness is to be practiced and sharpened over time and throughout one's lifetime.

The steady stream of giving should be from savings they have specifically set aside for the purpose of giving for he said, "let every one of you lay by him."

He also taught them to improve in their giving. The first thing he taught them was that they were to start from giving from their abundance, for it was "as God hath prospered him." Later, he uses the example of the Macedonians to teach them the riches of liberality, which is often sacrificial. Thus, while the understanding of the grace of the Lord Jesus inspires sacrificial giving in the saints, it is not the only form of giving Paul taught the saints.

We can learn some lessons from how the saints practiced the riches of liberality:

> *27. And in these days came prophets from Jerusalem unto Antioch. 28. And there stood up one of them named Agabus, and signified by the Spirit that there should be great dearth throughout all the world: which came to pass in the days of Claudius Caesar. 29. Then the disciples, every man according to his ability, determined to send relief unto the brethren which dwelt in Judaea: 30. Which also they did, and sent it to the elders by the hands of Barnabas and Saul.*
>
> *Acts 11:27 - 30*

Observe Agabus' prophecy:

Prophet Agabus "signified by the Spirit that there should be great dearth throughout all the world". He did not interpret that prophecy nor did he instruct the saints on what to do with that prophecy. Agabus did not prophesy financial increase or promise financial breakthrough to those who responded to that prophecy.

He simply let them know what was about to happen.

Agabus did not attempt to govern the church through prophecy.

It was after Agabus had finished giving his prophecy that the saints agreed what it meant and how they would respond.

When the disciples heard of Agabus' prophecy that "there should be great dearth throughout all the world", they did not spend their time trying to stop the dearth. They did not interpret it to mean that it was the sins of the brethren at Judea that had brought on the dearth. This earth is governed by economic highs and lows, which come and go in cycles. The saints had been taught to express the riches of liberality towards the Judean saints.

The prophets did not induce the saints at Antioch to give by telling them to use their financial gifts to plug into the "anointing" operating in the ministries of these prophets. These prophets did not use the operation of the word of wisdom to draw money from the pocket of the saints at Antioch.

Observe how the saints acted on Agabus' prophecy:

They responded to the prophecy as individuals but they administered their response as a body of saints. No one took a personal trip to execute the response to Agabus' prophecy. It was "every man according to his ability", which means that each purposed to contribute in the local assembly. Luke shows that it was as an assembly that they pooled their giving together for Barnabas and Paul to take to the saints in need at Jerusalem.

This is instructive.

Although Barnabas and Paul delivered the liberality of the saints at Antioch to the saints at Jerusalem, Barnabas and Paul did not go from house to house in Jerusalem looking for the saints to give to. Luke says they "sent it to the elders". Thus, the riches of the liberality of the saints of Antioch was administered to the Jerusalem saints as they assembled in their fellowship meetings at Jerusalem. Both the expression of the riches of liberality and the reception of it were in the local church.

The record in the book of Acts is that the practice of the saints when giving to those in need was that:

The saints expressing the riches of liberality purpose in their heart according to their ability.

No promises were made about material blessings coming back to those who expressed the riches of liberality.

All those expressing the riches of liberality pooled their generous gifts together in their assemblies.

The saints then give the pooled gifts to the Elders in their own local assemblies.

The Elders in the local assemblies expressing the riches of liberality then gave the gifts to the elders in the assemblies that received the gifts.

The Elders in the local assemblies receiving the riches of liberality then distribute to the saints in need at the receiving assemblies.

It is implied that the practice of the riches of generosity depended on the saints coming together in fellowship – in order to express the riches of liberality and to receive the riches of liberality from others.

Giving to other saints as an expression of the riches of generosity is a practice of the local church.

This was the practice of the Philippians:

18. But I have all, and abound: I am full, having received of Epaphroditus the things which were sent from you, an odour of a sweet smell, a sacrifice acceptable, wellpleasing to God.
Philippians 4:18

Paul received the things which the Philippians sent through Epaphroditus.

Epaphroditus was the "priest" that supplied the sweet-smelling sacrifice to Paul. Paul referred to Epaphroditus as "my brother, and companion in labour, and fellowsoldier, but your messenger." Thus, Epaphroditus was a messenger or apostle from the Philippians to Paul (see Philippians 2:25). Paul clearly held Epaphroditus in the highest esteem. He told the Philippians, "hold such in reputation: Because for the work of Christ he was nigh unto death, not regarding his life (see Philippians 2:29 - 30).

We know that these Philippians were the Macedonians that Paul bragged to the Corinthians about because Philippi is the "chief city of that part of Macedonia" (see Acts 16:12, Philippians 4:15). Therefore, Philippians were one of the churches of Macedonia who were in deep poverty (see 2 Corinthians 2:1-2) and yet they were Paul's greatest financial supporters (see Philippians 4:15-16).

The pattern in Antioch is seen in Philippians:

The saints at Philippi did not give individually to Paul.

They pooled their gifts together as an assembly. They must have given it to the Elders who then sent it through Epaphroditus, who was one of the Elders.

Paul wanted the saints to know how their gifts got to him – it was through Epaphroditus.

Paul wanted the saints to know how their gifts got to him – it was through Epaphroditus.

Paul did not promise Epaphroditus immunity to sickness on account of Epaphroditus' giving – in fact he confirmed that Epaphroditus fell sick as a result of the physical hardship and overwork involved in getting the gift to Paul.

This fact that Paul received the gift from the church is important. Paul received from the church because he ministered to the church. Getting their gift to the recipient as a gift from the local assembly implies that the saints placed a higher premium on the expression of the riches of liberality than they did on competing to be the recognized giver-in chief.

1 Moreover, brethren, we do you to wit of the grace of God bestowed on the churches of Macedonia; 2 how that in a great trial of affliction, the abundance of their joy and their deep poverty abounded unto the riches of their liberality.
2 Corinthians 8:1-2

Paul mentioned the riches of the liberality of the Macedonians to the Corinthians.

It wasn't individuals but the whole church giving as one.

Why did Paul tell the Corinthians of the liberality of the Macedonians?

I speak not by commandment, but by occasion of the forwardness of others, and to prove the sincerity of your love.
2 Corinthians 8:8

Paul used the expression of the riches of the Macedonians' liberality to provoke the Corinthians to follow the example of the Macedonians by expressing the riches of good works.

In true apostolic fashion, no promises were made about material blessings coming back to the Macedonians on account of expressing the riches of liberality.

Paul taught that the riches of liberality seen in the Macedonians is proof of the same riches in the Corinthians.

1 Now concerning the collection for the saints, as I have given order to the churches of Galatia, even so do ye. 2 Upon the first day of the week let every one of you lay by him in store, as God hath prospered him, that there be no gatherings when I come. 3 And when I come, whomsoever ye shall approve by your letters, them will I send to bring your liberality unto Jerusalem. 4 And if it be meet that I go also, they shall go with me.
1 Corinthians 16:1-4

In the KJV, God is italicized in "let every one of you lay by him in store, as God hath prospered him." God is inserted in italics because Paul did not mention God at all in the verse.

The Amplified reads:

"On the first day of every week each one of you is to put something aside, in proportion to his prosperity, and save it so that no collections [will need to] be made when I come."

J.B. Phillips reads:

"On the first day of the week let everyone put so much by him, according to his financial ability, so that there will be no need for collections when I come."

The NIV reads:

"On the first day of every week, each one of you should set aside a sum of money in keeping with your income, saving it up, so that when I come no collections will have to be made."

Paul wasn't saying God prospers people financially to various degrees. His point was that giving should be proportional to material riches. The prosperity that God gives is the riches of liberality in His saints. He gives equally to all saints.

Again, we see the same pattern in Antioch and Philippians repeated amongst the Corinthians.

This gives us more detail about the practice of the riches of liberality than we have seen elsewhere.

Paul's words to the Corinthians were, "that there be no gatherings when I come" (v2).

This validates the fact that the saints pooled their giving together before they administered it. Paul instructed that the pooling together of material resources was to be in Paul's absence.

How would the gifts get to those in need?

Paul said, "when I come, whomsoever ye shall approve by your letters, them will I send to bring your liberality unto Jerusalem" (v3).

The liberality of the Corinthians will get to Jerusalem via Elders approved amongst the Corinthians.

Then Paul said, "and if it be meet that I go also, they shall go with me" (v4).

If occasion allowed, Paul would take the Corinthian gifts to Jerusalem, together with the Corinthian Elders, on behalf of the Corinthian saints. Thus, it wasn't always the most senior of the Elders that took the gift.

Things were not covered in a cloak of mystery. The people knew the gifts would get to those who needed it and how it would get there.

8

Even as your Soul Prospereth

The prayers that we find in the epistles tell us a lot about the men that prayed them. Our emphasis in our prayers for other people inform us about where we are in our spiritual walk. John's prayer for Gaius would give us valuable insight.

2. Beloved, I wish above all things that thou mayest prosper and be in health, even as thy soul prospereth.
3 John 1:2

The word translated "wish" carries the force of a desire. This desire has been voiced as a prayer. Therefore, it is correct to translate wish as "pray" in this instance.

The word "prosper" or a variant of it occurs twice in this single verse. Almost all agree that the word translated "prospers" in "even as your soul prospers" refers to spiritual prosperity. However, there is disagreement over the meaning of "prosper" in "prosper and be in health". On account of those two words "prosper" and "prospers", many say that Apostle John is praying for material wealth to abound in Gaius.

Some say that "even as" in "prosper and be in health, even as thy soul prospereth" implies that John is showing us the secret formula by which one type of prosperity causes the other. These teach that spiritual growth produces material riches. They propose that God wants His children to grow spiritually so that He can place massive material riches in their care. This way, they are not destroyed by the great abundance placed in their trust. In this light, God's ultimate aim is the material riches He puts in the care of His saints and spiritual growth is a mechanism for qualifying for being entrusted with the riches of this world.

Some teach that prosperity promises planted in the mind are reaped as harvest of material riches. This they term the prosperity of the soul. Therefore, if we are unhappy with our financial situation we are to examine our mindset about money, plant the right prosperity scriptures, water it with prayer and reap financial promotion. They see in John's prayer for Gaius, a promise or formula for manifesting wealth.

In approaching John's prayer for Gaius, we are to observe the following characteristics of the epistles:

Asides from the book of Romans, the apostles generally write the epistles to respond to questions that have been posed by their hearers.

The Epistles generally open with a greeting followed by thanksgiving. This thanksgiving almost always focuses on the spiritual soundness as well as riches in the saints to whom the epistles are addressed. These riches are always spiritual in nature.

After the opening greetings and thanksgiving, we have the body of the epistle with the exhortation or the message, which then close off in a manner similar to the opening greeting. We observe that in the opening or closing portions the apostles often state their wish towards the saints in the churches that are the recipients of the particular epistle.

As an example, Paul's opening lines in Ephesians:

3. Blessed be the God and Father of our Lord Jesus Christ, who hath blessed us with all spiritual blessings in heavenly places in Christ:
Ephesians 1:3

The greeting and thanksgiving in Paul's opening lines assures the saints that the spirit is God's blessing given by Christ's sacrifice. The saint is not promised anything.

It is noteworthy that if we suppress the second verse in 3rd John, the whole letter reads as one continuous thought, lacking in the idea that John was referring to the acquisition of wealth or material riches. This should make us examine the second verse more closely.

What's the meaning of John's prosperity?

Beloved, I wish above all things that thou mayest prosper and be in health, even as thy soul prospereth.
3 John 1:2

We aim to arrive at the meaning of Bible words in line with the context in which they are used. We get into trouble when we fix meanings independent of context.

The Greek verb translated "prosper" is a compound word meaning "to have a good road" or "to have a successful path ahead of you". Thus, it easily translates to having a successful journey.

The word translated "prosper" in 3 John 2 is also used in 1 Corinthians 16:2. Paul used "prosper" in a financial way in his letter to the Corinthians:

2. Upon the first day of the week let every one of you lay by him in store, as God hath prospered him, that there be no gatherings when I come.
1 Corinthians 16:2

In this Corinthian passage the word "prospered" means financial prosperity.

We can better understand the full import of 1 Corinthians 16:2 by considering 1 Corinthians 16:3.

3. And when I come, whomsoever ye shall approve by your letters, them will I send to bring your liberality unto Jerusalem.
1 Corinthians 16:3

Paul clarifies and amplifies the "prosper" and shows that his emphasis was the liberality of the saints. The saint that makes progress and succeeds in financial affairs should let it be an avenue to express the riches of liberality.

The word translated "prosper" in 3 John 2 is also used in Romans 1:10.

10. Making request, if by any means now at length I might have a prosperous journey by the will of God to come unto you.
Romans 1: 10

In this passage in Romans, "I might have a prosperous journey" is one word. Paul used the word "prosper" to mean "to accomplish or finish without hiccups" or to "progress as one would on a journey". Paul anticipates a safe journey that won't involve his usual dose of persecution. He wants things working out well so that he could visit the saints in Rome. Here, Paul's "prosper" doesn't mean material abundance. The word prosper isn't exclusively concerned with financial prosperity.

John's "above all things" means "as touching or concerning all things". It would be all these things that John writes to Gaius about in 3 John.

If we'd read the verses prior to and after the verse in question, we can fix the meaning of the notorious second verse. As we read through the whole of 3 John, we see that he had taken pains to explain the intent of the words that he used in the second verse.

Here are the verses that immediately surround verse 2:

3. For I rejoiced greatly, when the brethren came and testified of the truth that is in thee, even as thou walkest in the truth. 4. I have no greater joy than to hear that my children walk in truth. 5. Beloved, thou doest faithfully whatsoever thou doest to the brethren, and to strangers;
3 John 1:3 – 5

John said, "the brethren came and testified of the truth that is in thee". John's prayer in the second verse was on account of the testimony of the brethren who had seen evidences of the truth in Gaius.

Now we know that when John said he rejoiced greatly concerning Gaius, the object of John's rejoicing was that Gaius was walking in the truth to such a degree that other brethren could testify of it.

2. For the truth's sake, which dwelleth in us, and shall be with us for ever.
2 John 1:2

John's truth was the indwelling of God in us by His spirit. This is the power of God's love in His saints.

18. My little children, let us not love in word, neither in tongue; but in deed and in truth.
1 John 3:18

The deed of that truth is the love walk. This is the riches of liberality.

Thus, John's greatest joy was to hear that Gaius was walking in the truth. Gaius excelled in the riches of good conduct by which he blessed the saints. John's truth referred to Gaius doing "faithfully whatsoever thou doest to the brethren" (see 3 John 1:2 – 5).

Be in health

The word translated "health" can refer to physical healing:

10. And they that were sent, returning to the house, found the servant whole that

had been sick.
Luke 7:10

The word translated "health" in 3 John 1:2 has been translated whole. This refers to physical healing.

Health can also figuratively refer to the New Birth:

31. And Jesus answering said unto them, They that are whole need not a physician; but they that are sick. 32. I came not to call the righteous, but sinners to repentance.
Luke 5:31 – 32

The word translated health in 3 John 1:2 has been translated "whole" in this verse. Jesus wasn't discussing bodily health. Jesus' "they that are whole need not a physician" was a figure of speech referring to those Pharisees. He said the Pharisees were "they which justify yourselves before men" (see Luke 16:15). He was saying the Pharisees assumed that they had righteousness before men. If they had been righteous, they would have been cooperating with Jesus in reaching out to sinners. Their condemnation of sinners showed they were not righteous. In reality, the Pharisees were also sinners in need of repentance. Jesus was using irony, mixed with humour and sarcasm.

Therefore, the sick were the sinners who needed to repent.

Since both the Pharisees and the sinners needed to repent, Jesus had come to call all to repentance. The Pharisees were not excluded from salvation except by their refusal to repent. Once they repent, they receive salvation, which is wholeness. Jesus is the physician who supplies salvation as healing or soundness. By a figure of speech, the New Birth is health.

In the Epistles, the word translated "health," when addressed to ministers, is used exclusively in a spiritual sense to refer to good doctrine:

1. But speak thou the things which become sound doctrine: 2. That the aged men

be sober, grave, temperate, sound in faith, in charity, in patience.
Titus 2:1 - 2

The word translated health in 3 John 1:2 has been translated sound in "sound doctrine" in verse 1 and sound in "sound in faith in charity, in patience" in verse 2.

Health or soundness refers to purity of doctrine in verse 1 and to a spiritual testimony void of error in verse 2. They were to have a sound spiritual walk.

This meaning of health as a reference to spiritual soundness or doctrinal soundness is evident in Paul's letter to Timothy:

13. Hold fast the form of sound words, which thou hast heard of me, in faith and love which is in Christ Jesus.
2 Timothy 1:13

The word translated health in 3 John 2 has been translated sound in "sound words". This is a reference to sound doctrine devoid of error (see also 2 Timothy 4:3, and 1 Timothy 6:2-3).

John said:

"… even as thou walkest in the truth" (see 3 John 1:3).

"… to hear that my children walk in truth" (see 3 John 1:4).

Thus, the use of "health" in John's epistle is in keeping with how the Apostles used it when writing to elders. The "health" in "thou mayest prosper and be in health, even as thy soul prospereth", refers to being sound, complete and free from doctrinal error.

As the later verses show, "be in health" refers to walking in the truth instead of yielding to error. So, we see that John's use of "health" was not a reference to bodily healing. John rejoiced in the soundness of Gaius' conduct towards other saints and ministers who brought back testimony of his walk.

The expression "be in health" referred to Gaius' soundness concerning the truth. It means Gaius was to continue to grow spiritually. John meant that Gaius wasn't walking contrary to the gospel by stepping out of love in his conduct towards other saints and ministers. Gaius wasn't mixing worldliness, covetousness and selfishness. He was operating in contentment.

Although there is nothing wrong with saints acquiring material possessions, that isn't what John was rejoicing about.

As thy soul prospereth

The word soul has a wide variety of meaning in scripture. It is used to represent the physical life of a person or animal; an individual person; as well as attitudes, emotions, feelings, and thoughts. We shouldn't be quick to assume it refers to the human mind all the time.

38. Now the just shall live by faith: but if any man draw back, my soul shall have no pleasure in him
Hebrews 10:38

God refers to Himself as a soul. He means His person.

41. Then they that gladly received his word were baptized: and the same day there were added unto them about three thousand souls.
Acts 2:41

Referring to these three thousand souls, Luke says, "they continued steadfastly in the apostles' doctrine and fellowship, and in breaking of bread, and in prayers" (see Acts 2:42). Therefore, these souls broke bread, prayed, and fellowshipped with other saints. It is clear that these souls referred to the whole person. Luke meant that three thousand people received eternal life.

20. Which sometime were disobedient, when once the longsuffering of God waited in the days of Noah, while the ark was a preparing, wherein few, that is,

eight souls were saved by water.
1 Peter 3:20

The eight souls that were saved in Noah's day were not eight minds roaming in the mental realm without a body. The writer of Hebrews clarifies that Noah "prepared an ark to the saving of his house" (see Hebrews 11:7). The souls referred to full people and not to minds. These are the members of Noah's household. It is eight lives that were preserved physically.

19. And I will say to my soul, Soul, thou hast much goods laid up for many years; take thine ease, eat, drink, and be merry.
Luke 12:19

The rich fool has a soul that possessed much goods.

This soul could eat, drink and be merry.

The use of soul here helps us anticipate that more than the mind is intended. Whatever this "soul" is, it should at least involve the physical body since it is the physical body that eats and drinks. Soul here is the whole person.

We see that many times, the word "soul" is used to refer to the total person – mind, body and spirit taken together. John is not referring to Gaius' mind but Gaius' well-being – the whole man. To stay true to the overall tone of John's Epistle, the soul would be a reference to Gaius' whole spiritual life. The soul prospering would refer to the soundness in spiritual walk, which is what it means to "be in health".

The tag of "difficult text" that we have forced upon John's writing is vanishing. It wasn't the text that was troublesome, it was our desire to see material wealth as the apostle's prayer that was troublesome. This trouble is man-made.

In 3 John 1:2, John was no more talking about bodily healing than he was talking about financial prosperity. He was praying that Gaius was to be so fully developed spiritually that the testimony of the brethren about the truth in him would continue.

What was John praying about?

John's prayer teaches us to pray that saints prosper (complete the journey towards being sound spiritually). This means that we pour out our lives in prayer for other saints as we prioritize their spiritual health measured through their lives mirroring the truth that is within them through the New Birth. These saints prosper in the good works that they do to the brethren.

Do we have any other example of any apostle praying this way for saints to grow spiritually by their grasp of revelation knowledge?

Let's learn from examples of New Testament slants in prayer

Paul's prayer for Philemon:

4. I thank my God, making mention of thee always in my prayers, 5. Hearing of thy love and faith, which thou hast toward the Lord Jesus, and toward all saints; 6. That the communication of thy faith may become effectual by the acknowledging of every good thing which is in you in Christ Jesus. 7. For we have great joy and consolation in thy love, because the bowels of the saints are refreshed by thee, brother.
Philemon 1:4 - 7

Paul knew of Philemon's love and faith towards all saints. He then prayed the prayer in verse 6 about the riches of acknowledging every good thing in Philemon in Christ. Communication is fellowship, which describes supply. It is a two-fold supply. Firstly, it reminds of God supplying Christ as His riches in Philemon. Paul's prayer was for Philemon to acknowledge the riches of God so that, the saint becomes more fruitful in that knowledge. Secondarily, it is Philemon communicating that capacity to share in the form of ministry. This is Philemon making spiritual progress. The result of that prayer is God's riches showing up as Philemon's ministry of refreshing the bowels of the saints. Philemon would supply his love walk as his spiritual sacrifice to Onesimus. This is the riches of mercy.

Paul's prayer for the Philippians:

9. And this I pray, that your love may abound yet more and more in knowledge and in all judgment; 10. That ye may approve things that are excellent; that ye may be sincere and without offence till the day of Christ;
Philippians 1:9 - 10

Paul prayed that the love may abound in knowledge. He means that the knowledge of God's great love in Christ would cause the love walk of the saints to abound so that the saints are without offense. In like manner, John would pray that the Philippians should be "in health."

We observe in these examples that the emphasis of the prayers in the epistles was about the discovery of the Father's character through the work of His Son, God's riches in the saints and the saint awakening to that mighty supply.

Failing to understand the way the apostles prayed, we project our emphasis in prayer unto theirs. For as long as we fail to prioritize God's riches in Christ, it will not show in our prayers – we find ourselves praying for things the apostles did not pray for.

The apostle John prayed for Gaius to prosper in that same "prosperity" that Paul prayed for the saints.

John clarified what he meant by "prosper and be in health, even as thy soul prospereth". He told Gaius:

11. Beloved, follow not that which is evil, but that which is good. He that doeth good is of God: but he that doeth evil hath not seen God.
3 John 1:11

John had heard of Gaius' spiritual testimony, so he prayed that Gaius would make further progress and remain sound.

The proper name for the prosperity of 3 John 1:2 is the prosperity called spiritual growth, which is evidenced in the supply of the riches of good works that we do to other saints. Gaius' grasp of and progress in that truth of God's love

Gaius was to grow spiritually by paying heed to the truth of the riches of God's love that was already in him. He was to give expression to the riches of kindness and liberality because God had placed that power in his life. Gaius would display the riches of a sound love walk. Gaius was to develop in the soundness of ministering to other saints. He wasn't to adulterate that soundness by adding erroneous practices to it.

John told Gaius of the words of his prayer to strengthen Gaius' soundness so that the saint would be very clear about the prayer and what the answer to the prayer would look like. John's words explain what prospering and being in health, even as the soul prospereth looks like and what it is not.

Demetrius was another example of prospering and being in health, even as the soul prospereth (see 3 John 1:12).

Diotrephes, who loveth to have the pre-eminence among them, receiveth us not (see 3 John 1:9), was an example of not being in health – mixing the error of selfishness with God's salvation.

How did the brethren testify of "the truth that is in" Gaius?

6. Which have borne witness of thy charity before the church: whom if thou bring forward on their journey after a godly sort, thou shalt do well:
3 John 1:6

John clarified the brethren's testimony that he had mentioned in verse *3. He said that these brethren have "borne witness of thy charity before the church".*

The word translated "before" in "thy charity before the church" is a word that means "before their eyes" or in their presence.

The answer to John's prayer for Gaius was that he would continue in the good work of bringing the saints forward on their journey.

5. Beloved, thou doest faithfully whatsoever thou doest to the brethren, and to strangers (see 3 John 1:5).

Although many use 3 John 1:2 as justification for praying that saints prosper financially, the prosperity that John is talking about is not financial, it is the riches of completing the journey towards spiritual soundness.

9

Amazed at His doctrine

When asked to interpret the teaching of the holy scriptures, Jesus explained that the message which preceded the Law and which the Law tried to convey is that of believing God's love and loving men (which is the corresponding action of that belief – see Matthew 22:35 – 40). This two-fold message of faith and love is the message contained within those portions of the holy scriptures that spoke of Christ. Jesus' explanation shows that all what Moses tried to teach was men loving God with their heart (believing unto righteousness) and loving the brethren (the consequence of believing God's love)

When the teachers heard His profound explanation "no man was able to answer him a word" (see Matthew 22:46). Nobody could deny the truth of His explanation.

Earlier Jesus had said,

17. Think not that I am come to destroy the law, or the prophets: I am not come to destroy, but to fulfil.
Matthew 5:17

Then Jesus began a series of "you have heard it said … but I say" dialogues. He was acting out what fulfilling the Law and prophets meant. In context, Jesus fulfilled the Law and prophets by His explanations which clarified the true intent of the message hidden within the Law and prophets.

The law or the prophets refer to the holy scriptures. Jesus means that the great challenge with the scriptures is with how it has been explained by those who teach it. In the context of Matthew 5, Jesus fulfilled the Law and the Prophets by His explanations which clarified the true intent of the message hidden within the Law and the Prophets.

Again, we see the effect of Jesus' explanation:

1. At that time Jesus went on the sabbath day through the corn; and his disciples were an hungred, and began to pluck the ears of corn, and to eat. 2. But when the Pharisees saw it, they said unto him, Behold, thy disciples do that which is not lawful to do upon the sabbath day. 3. But he said unto them, Have ye not read what David did, when he was an hungred, and they that were with him; 4. How he entered into the house of God, and did eat the shewbread, which was not lawful for him to eat, neither for them which were with him, but only for the priests? 5. Or have ye not read in the law, how that on the sabbath days the priests in the temple profane the sabbath, and are blameless? 6. But I say unto you, That in this place is one greater than the temple.7. But if ye had known what this meaneth, I will have mercy, and not sacrifice, ye would not have condemned the guiltless.

Matthew 12:1 - 7

The Pharisees explained the scriptures as teaching that the act of plucking the ears of corn to eat on the Sabbath day was unlawful. In response, Jesus said, "Have ye not read what David did?" He meant that the Pharisees had not understood what they read in scriptures therefore their explanations were incorrect. Jesus explained David's action and that of the priests who did the unlawful and His interpretation of those texts in the same holy scriptures was that they meant that God desires mercy and not sacrifice! The Pharisees' explanation had imposed burdens that produced bondage in their hearers. Jesus' explanations show that the burden imposed by the Pharisee was a revelation of their hearts' departure from God's love and mercy. The hardness seen in the Pharisees' interpretation did not proceeded from or reveal God. It showed that those Pharisees were hard hearted.

Jesus' explanation meant that David ate the shewbread to quench his hunger because he was a believer in God's mercy, and knew what Moses was trying to teach.

Also, the priests in the temple profane the Sabbath on the Sabbath days and are blameless because they knew that those ordinances were just teaching tools.

In the explanation of Jesus, we find that the Pharisees did not believe God's mercy.

After hearing Jesus' clear explanation of God's mercy from the scriptures they had used to hold men in bondage, the "Pharisees went out, and held a council against him, how they might destroy him" (see Matthew 12:14). Jesus explained why they did this. He said, "an evil man out of the evil treasure bringeth forth evil things" (see Matthew 12:35). The explanation of the Pharisees were the evil things they brought forth from their evil heart. In Hebrews, this is called "an evil heart of unbelief, in departing from the living God" (see Hebrews 3:12).

The Pharisees had an evil heart of unbelief. Their wrong interpretation, based on unbelief, meant that they used the instructions which Moses' meant to use to teach mercy to enslave men. They abandoned divine revelation and used its words to teach the commandments of men. They taught heavy rituals but failed to arrive at faith and love.

Peter confirmed that the interpretation of the Law as commandments for men to fulfil for salvation or sanctification was a burden none could bear (see Acts 15:10).

The Pharisees' interpretation of the Law imposed a burden on their hearers rather than leading them to faith in Christ. This was because their interpretation was contrary to Moses' intent.

How did the people react to Jesus' explanation of scriptures?

And all the people were amazed, and said, Is not this the son of David? (see Matthew 12:23).

I am not come to destroy, but to fulfil

Jesus began a series of "you have heard it said … but I say" dialogues by which He gave clear examples of how to interpret and explain Genesis to Malachi:

43. Ye have heard that it hath been said, Thou shalt love thy neighbour, and hate thine enemy. 44. But I say unto you, Love your enemies, bless them that curse you, do good to them that hate you, and pray for them which despitefully use you, and persecute you; 45. That ye may be the children of your Father which is in heaven: for he maketh his sun to rise on the evil and on the good, and sendeth rain on the just and on the unjust.
Matthew 5:43 - 45

Jesus' explanation showed that God's way was to love His enemies, bless them that curse or speak evil of Him and do good to them that hate Him. So, "hate thine enemy" is not God's commandment, it is the commandment of men. It is unbelieving men that explained God's commandment of love as a demand to hate! Jesus fulfilled the law by using His explanations to separate what belonged to God and what did not.

In the Sermon on the Mount, Jesus used plain speech as He took texts from Genesis to Malachi and explained them to show God's true nature from the same texts that the unbelieving Pharisees had used to prevent their hearers from seeing God as He truly is.

In Jesus' explanation, we find that those aspects of Moses' teaching that appear as opposite to God's love are not God's commands, but Moses' way of exposing the hardness of man's heart. God's will is mercy and not sacrifice. It is men that condemn (see Matthew 12:7). God's command is faith and love (see Matthew 22:35 – 40).

45. Do not think that I will accuse you to the Father: there is one that accuseth you, even Moses, in whom ye trust. 46. For had ye believed Moses, ye would have believed me: for he wrote of me.
John 5:45 - 46

Jesus' explanation shed phenomenal light on Moses' teaching ministry. There was a portion of Moses' teachings that were to be believed for they spoke of Christ. For those that failed to believe Moses but trusted in their own performance, he also wrote other things that accused them. Moses accused them for their sin of not believing what he had written about Jesus.

Thus, in Jesus' explanations we understand Moses' words "I have set before thee this day life and good, and death and evil" (see Deuteronomy 30: 15). "Life and good" is Moses' ministry of things to believe about Jesus, while "death and evil" is his ministry of accusation for not believing. Moses set both messages side by side and they often coincided.

The hardness of your hearts

Jesus gave insight into why Moses wrote those teachings that were not faith-giving:

In answer to the Pharisee's query, "why did Moses then command to give a writing of divorcement, and to put her away?", Jesus responded, "Moses because of the hardness of your hearts suffered you to put away your wives: but from the beginning it was not so" (see Matthew 19:7 - 8). That hard heart is the unbelief of men. Some of Moses' words that the Pharisees had taken as commandments were in fact not commandments but Moses' attempt to reveal to men the hardness in their heart. He was showing them that they had departed from God's love. Moses documented the unbelief that was in the heart of men.

43. Ye have heard that it hath been said, Thou shalt love thy neighbour, and hate thine enemy. 44. But I say unto you, Love your enemies, bless them that curse you, do good to them that hate you, and pray for them which despitefully use

you, and persecute you;
Matthew 5:43 - 44

In the light of Moses' two-fold message, "Thou shalt love thy neighbour" is Moses' teaching God's commandment of love, while "hate thine enemy" is the response of the hardness of man's heart. Jesus clarifies God's command as "I say to you, love your enemies". In effect, when David killed Goliath "in the name of the Lord", David showed the extent to which his heart was hardened towards expressing God's love nature to others.

This would mean that God had not demanded the death of men like Goliath and Pharaoh. Men had killed their enemies in response to their own hard heart or the hard heart of others. In Jesus' explanation, God is conspicuous by His absence. The idea of hating their enemies was the commandments of men. It was man-made.

When Jesus said, "bless them that curse you, do good to them that hate you, and pray for them which despitefully use you, and persecute you", He was using what God is like to describe what His saints would be like.

45. That ye may be the children of your Father which is in heaven:
Matthew 5:45

Jesus explained that man does not have to reciprocate in kind but in opposites because that is God's way. Once He establishes what God is like, we know and discover God's attributes in His saints. Thus, we do not bless in order to be like God. His point is that we are as God and the proof is that we bless them that curse us, do good to them that hate us and pray for them which despitefully use us, and persecute us.

48. Be ye therefore perfect, even as your Father which is in heaven is perfect.
Matthew 5:48

Jesus explained the faith-giving words of the prophets to be teachings of the Father's perfection.

The perfection of God is His unconditional love. Were He a man, He would bless them that curse Him, do good to them that hate Him and pray for those that despitefully used Him. When a man only loves as a payback for love received from others, such a man is not in the perfection of God. God's perfection is His love as a disposition of His nature and not as a consequence of the merit of the other party.

Jesus' expression, "he maketh his sun to rise on the evil and on the good, and sendeth rain on the just and on the unjust" means that God does not reciprocate man's hatred with His own hatred. He continues to show mercy even to our enemies. Jesus was not commenting on trade, commerce, or wealth creation. He teaches that God does not return fire for fire. Thus, God would have spared the people that were killed under the guise of God's supposed command in the holy scriptures. Those who died in the hands of the people of God had not been shown the mercy of God. Goliath's death was David's wrath in action. God's mercy was not allowed to prevail.

The Sermon on the Mount is a prophecy of the way the new creation man would live. Rather than hating enemies, as people who have believed the gospel, we love our enemies, bless them that curse us, do good to them that hate us, and pray for them which despitefully use us, and persecute us. This is the way of our heavenly Father.

Jesus clarifies the meaning and intent of scriptural text.

He taught them as one having authority

28. And it came to pass, when Jesus had ended these sayings, the people were astonished at his doctrine: 29. For he taught them as one having authority, and not as the scribes.

Matthew 7:28 - 29

The series of explanations that had started with the Sermon on the Mount in Matthew 5 continued in a steady stream all the way through to Matthew 7:27 as one continuous teaching. The effect on the people who heard him was that they were astonished at his doctrine because "he taught them as one having authority, and not as the scribes".

Jesus' authority is the particular (and biased) way that He explained the scriptures to clarify the Father's nature. He tackled millennia-old misconceptions about godliness (what God is like) and He explained the sacred scriptures to bring out God's true character. The scribes' interpretation of the same scriptures hid the love of God while teaching their traditions and by so doing robbed the scriptures of its power to reveal God. Jesus said unto the Pharisees and the scribes, "Full well ye reject the commandment of God, that ye may keep your own tradition (see Mark 7:9). He meant that they were hypocritical in that while they picked their texts from scriptures, their explanations rejected the very truth of those scriptures they were quoting! Rather than teach sound doctrine, the scribes simply repeated what tradition demanded. Paul called this form of communication "old wives' fables" while Peter called it "cunningly devised fables" (see 2 Peter 1:16).

Those that listened to Jesus were astonished at His doctrine or the way He explained the Genesis to Malachi text.

In Capernaum, the response to Jesus' teaching was, "they questioned among themselves, saying, What thing is this? what new doctrine is this?" (see Mark 1:21-27). Those that heard Jesus exclaimed, "what new doctrine is this?" He did not bring another Bible. It was His explanation that was new to them. The doctrine of Christ is not like the doctrine of the Pharisees and of the Sadducees. Since in context, He was casting out demons, it must have been His explanation of the casting out of demons that shocked them. Until we come in contact with the ministry of Jesus, a superficial reading of Genesis through Malachi makes it look like evil spirits come from God (see 1 Samuel 16:14-15, 23).

In another place, He explains the difference between His teachings and that of the Pharisees and Sadducees:

> *11. How is it that ye do not understand that I spake it not to you concerning bread, that ye should beware of the leaven of the Pharisees and of the*

Sadducees? 12. Then understood they how that he bade them not beware of the leaven of bread, but of the doctrine of the Pharisees and of the Sadducees.
Matthew 16:11 – 12

Jesus' "leaven of the Pharisees and of the Sadducees" meant that the bread served by the Pharisees was their explanation of scriptures in ways that imposed a burden on their hearers when they should have repented by teaching the way Jesus taught. There is the Jesus mode of explaining scriptures which is radically different from the Sadducees and Pharisees communication of cunning fables from their explanation of the same text. Thus, in Genesis to Malachi faith and love are hidden. It is our job to follow the example of the Lord by continuing to explain those texts the same way that He interpreted them rather than the way of the scribes.

Which will you adopt?

As He was about to finish His sermon on the mount, the Lord said,

"Beware of false prophets, which come to you in sheep's clothing, but inwardly they are ravening wolves" (see Matthew 7:15).

Beware means be alert. Be on guard.

False prophets in sheep's clothing means that they come dressed as sheep. Sheep's clothing is wool. Peter said of false prophets "and through covetousness shall they with feigned words make merchandise of you" (see 2 Peter 2:3). True prophecy reveals Christ but the teachings of false prophets promote covetousness. These false prophets acquired the wool by merchandising the sheep and fleecing them. The fleecing is in their doctrine. It is the teaching ministries of the Sadducees, Pharisees and scribes that Jesus referred to as false prophecy.

A false prophet is assumed to be God's mouthpiece but speaks contrary to Jesus' excellent revelation of God's person. Jeremiah had pointed out centuries before "The prophets prophesy lies in my name: I sent them not, neither have I commanded them, neither spake unto them: they prophesy unto you a false vision and divination, and a thing of nought, and the deceit of their heart" (see Jeremiah 14:14). False prophets use God's word to say things about God that veil His true nature from their hearers. They preach the commandments of men. We serve the Lord by staying with what He has said and the way He explained it. When we depart from that form of doctrine preached by Christ, covetousness is inevitable. Soon, we make merchandise of our hearers.

The question is "which will you adopt?"

The reason for scripture

Here's what Paul told Timothy about the reason for scripture:

15. And that from a child thou hast known the holy scriptures, which are able to make thee wise unto salvation through faith which is in Christ Jesus. 16. All scripture is given by inspiration of God, and is profitable for doctrine, for reproof, for correction, for instruction in righteousness:
2 Timothy 3:15 - 16

Since the word translated "scripture" in "all scripture" is a word that means that which is written, Paul is referring to Genesis through Malachi.

The word translated "holy in "holy scriptures" is a word that means the setting apart of one thing from others as was used of the temple or holy of holies. Paul means that within the bible are things written which communicate faith. These are to be taken as different from others in that they teach salvation through faith in Christ.

The word translated "scriptures" in "holy scriptures" is not the same as "scripture" in "all scripture". The "scriptures" in "holy scriptures" are from the Greek gramma, which refers to the outcome of reading, which is the learning transmitted in reading what is written.

4. For whatsoever things were written aforetime were written for our learning,

that we through patience and comfort of the scriptures might have hope.
Romans 15:4

The outcome of reading the writings in ancient scriptures is so that we might increase learning.

The word translated "learning" in Romans 15 is the same word translated "doctrine" in 2 Timothy 3: 16, "teaching" in Romans 12:7 and learning or mastery of facts in Acts 26:24.

In the light of these, we know that Paul was telling Timothy that the outcome of the contents of the holy scriptures is doctrine, teaching, learning or mastery of facts.

In 2 Timothy 3:15, Paul is telling Timothy, "you have learned the content of those things which were written to communicate faith and the result is that you have learned salvation. In learning from me, you became skillful or gained mastery in how to see that salvation, which you have learnt, in different books of the bible. "

In 2 Timothy 3:16, Paul is telling Timothy, "you are saved, now get to understand that salvation thoroughly by observing those that taught you. The things that you have learnt from what is written in scriptures are profitable for teaching others."

16. All scripture is given by inspiration of God, and is profitable for doctrine, for reproof, for correction, for instruction in righteousness:
2 Timothy 3:16

Genesis through Malachi are the "inspiration of God" or what men wrote down from the understanding that God gave them of Himself. That understanding is for doctrine, reproof, correction, and for instruction in righteousness.

The doctrine of Christ in Genesis to Malachi are God's corrections that He gave to the ancient world so that those men could be instructed about the righteousness or right actions of God. In simple terms, amidst the confusion in the ancient world, God gave the scriptures because He wanted men to know what to attribute to Him. This is the ability God has planted in His word and brought to light in the doctrine of Christ.

Learning from Paul's learning

Festus recognized Paul's scriptures (gramma) or learning:

> *24. And as he thus spake for himself, Festus said with a loud voice, Paul, thou art beside thyself; much learning doth make thee mad.*
> *Acts 26:22 - 24*

Festus recognized "much learning" in Paul. The force of Paul's learning made Festus exclaim in a loud voice.

What was the learning that made Festus exclaim?

> *22. Having therefore obtained help of God, I continue unto this day, witnessing both to small and great, saying none other things than those which the prophets and Moses did say should come:*
> *23. That Christ should suffer, and that he should be the first that should rise from the dead, and should shew light unto the people, and to the Gentiles.*
> *Acts 26: 22 - 23*

Paul explained Christ as the message of faith which "the prophets and Moses did say should come". Although we find the words of angels in the writings of the prophets, just like Jesus, Paul focused exclusively on what the prophets said. He was silent on the words of angels.

What was the effect of Paul's gramma or learning on Festus and Agrippa?

> *28. Then Agrippa said unto Paul, Almost thou persuadest me to be a Christian.*
> *Acts 26:28*

Agrippa found in Paul's learning a persuasion that inspired Agrippa towards believing. This means that when properly explained, Moses' writings would persuade a man to be a Christian. The goal of the commandment is truly faith and love (see 1 Timothy 1:5). Explaining the bible in that biased way that brings out Christ as its content and meaning is "much learning". Festus recognized that Paul displayed a mastery of the facts of scripture in a way that was different from what the scribes and Pharisees preached.

Since Paul said, "I continue unto this day, witnessing both to small and great, saying none other things than those which the prophets and Moses did say should come" (see Acts 26:22), we also say none other things when we explain Genesis through Malachi. This implies that Genesis was the initial statement of the gospel and all other scriptures that follow were written to expound on that original teaching in Genesis. The other books that came after Genesis are to be explained in a way that agrees with Genesis. We find the full explanation of Genesis and the books that have attempted to explain Genesis in the epistles. This means that the epistles are not a different message from Genesis through Malachi.

Although we can see other things to teach in scriptures, the great task of ministering sound doctrine is to stick with the faith-giving teaching of Christ. Our explanation of the writings of the prophets must be done in a way that distinguish us from those who desire to be teachers of the law. Using the text of scriptures to teach the law is interpreting the text differently from the way Jesus and Paul interpreted those texts. Once we do that we would be using the text of the prophets to say what the prophets did not say!

Paul instructed Timothy to follow his example by not desiring to preach the law:

Neither give heed to fables

4. Neither give heed to fables and endless genealogies, which minister questions, rather than godly edifying which is in faith: so do. 5. Now the end of the commandment is charity out of a pure heart, and of a good conscience, and of

faith unfeigned: 6. From which some having swerved have turned aside unto vain jangling;
7. Desiring to be teachers of the law; understanding neither what they say, nor whereof they affirm.
1 Timothy 1:4 - 7

When we read the commandments of the holy scriptures our explanation of the holy scriptures should converge on the faith and the love of God.

Ministers who veer away from teaching love as the explanation of the commandments are speaking empty words. What they are saying is wrong because it is not in line with the love of God.

Paul's admonition to Timothy means that we are to pay close attention to what the minister says. Ministers that covet a reputation to preach the law instead of Christ as the fulfilment of the law, prove by that very desire that they do not understand the law that they desire to preach! The law was put in the bible, not to be taught as commandments to live up to but as a pointer to that which God is obligated to fulfill. Our part is to believe!

The pride of knowing nothing

3 If any man teach otherwise, and consent not to wholesome words, even the words of our Lord Jesus Christ, and to the doctrine which is according to godliness; 4 he is proud, knowing nothing, but doting about questions and strifes of words, whereof cometh envy, strife, railings, evil surmisings, 5 perverse disputings of men of corrupt minds, and destitute of the truth, supposing that gain is godliness: from such withdraw thyself.
1 Timothy 6:3-5

As a whole, Paul's letters to Timothy contain the strongest concentration of the words "doctrine" and "godliness" occurring together in a single letter in all of the New Testament text. The reason for Paul's letters to Timothy is that Timothy might appreciate the seriousness of sound doctrine.

Paul puts a red flag on men that "teach otherwise." He says that this "teaching otherwise" is not consenting "to wholesome words". The word translated "wholesome" means sound. Sound teaching aligns with "the words of our Lord Jesus Christ". "The words of our Lord Jesus Christ" means that there is a way that the Lord Jesus taught doctrine that is according to godliness or that correctly explains what God is like. When a minister does not consent to the way that Jesus taught the scriptures, such a minister is "proud, knowing nothing, but doting about questions and strifes of words"! Any approach of teaching scriptures that departs from the doctrine of Christ would breed covetousness and lead to teaching things that are "destitute of the truth." This leads down the slippery slope of teaching that "gain is godliness" or that godliness is a means to increasing material riches.

Although the NIV and many other versions don't have it, the manuscript used for the KJV, Amplified and others include a remedy from Paul that we withdraw ourselves from ministers whose mode of explaining scriptures does not follow that pattern established in Christ.

Teach no other doctrine

17. Now I beseech you, brethren, mark them which cause divisions and offences contrary to the doctrine which ye have learned; and avoid them.18. For they that are such serve not our Lord Jesus Christ, but their own belly; and by good words and fair speeches deceive the hearts of the simple.

Romans 16:17 - 18

The minister understands that Jesus has explained the prophecies of the holy scriptures with a specific pattern. We serve Christ by ensuring we follow that pattern and conclude as He has concluded. When we interpret scriptures contrary to the doctrine that we have already received through Paul, we are the ones causing divisions. "Good words and fair speeches" mean that when you read the ancient prophets that Jesus and His holy apostles have already explained, you must not become so slippery and shoddy that your own explanation of those texts forces you into making promises that neither the Lord Jesus nor His apostles made after reading the same texts. That creativity in delivery that results in making promises not found in the Lord's explanation only deceives the heart of the saints and shows that we do not serve Christ but our bellies! As ministers of doctrine, we serve the Lord by staying with what He has said.

Paul's remedy was "avoid them", which means to shun.

3. As I besought thee to abide still at Ephesus, when I went into Macedonia, that thou mightest charge some that they teach no other doctrine,
1 Timothy 1:3

Timothy had learned from Paul's ministry how not to teach God's word as fables. Timothy was to command that ministers should teach no other doctrine. They were not to follow the established explanation found on the lips of the Pharisees whom Jesus called false prophets. The minister of the gospel must not disagree with the explanations already established by Christ and his holy apostles.

13. Hold fast the form of sound words, which thou hast heard of me, in faith and love which is in Christ Jesus.
2 Timothy 1:13

The "form of sound words" is that doctrinal pattern that was taught so clearly by the apostles that those who believed the apostles believed both the content of their message and their pattern of teaching. They continued in this pattern and were to hold fast to it because by understanding it, they'll be able to discern bad doctrine. In that pattern, the saints knew how to tackle the holy scriptures.

The term "sound words" is a reference to sound doctrine devoid of error (see also 2 Timothy 4:3, and 1 Timothy 6:2-3).

Thus, the greatest danger is not that we have not been exposed to sound doctrine, it is that we are continually tempted to let go of sound doctrine. Paul's answer? The minister is to hold fast!

Our conclusions are to be in line with that form of teaching "which is in Christ Jesus". The Lord Jesus examined the scriptures and His teachings explained it in a pointed way that amplified faith and love.

There are many unruly and vain talkers

Paul's instructions to Timothy, about how to teach the word were not a special set of instructions. He told Titus the same:

> *9. Holding fast the faithful word as he hath been taught, that he may be able by sound doctrine both to exhort and to convince the gainsayers. 10. For there are many unruly and vain talkers and deceivers, specially they of the circumcision: 11. Whose mouths must be stopped, who subvert whole houses, teaching things which they ought not, for filthy lucre's sake.*
> *Titus 1:9 - 11*

The unruly ministers are those who do not follow the pattern called sound doctrine. Sound doctrine refers to that healthy way that the Lord displayed in interpreting and explaining the holy scriptures. Since there is a healthy way, it implies there is an unsound or unhealthy way of explaining scriptures. It is this unhealthy way that is referred to as false doctrine. The Jewish fables is the mode of explanation not found in Christ, thus they were commandments of men because their conclusions opposed that of the Lord Jesus. False doctrine leads to full-blown covetousness.

Ministers who do not teach according to the pattern seen in the teachings of Paul which was based on that seen in the Lord are referred to as 'opposers'. These ministers oppose the very truth they assume they are teaching. Those who minister this way are called "unruly and vain talkers and deceivers". He pointed out "they of the circumcision" as noted examples of unruly and vain talkers.

He is describing the danger of desiring to teach the law.

We see a recurring theme of "filthy lucre's sake" in the mode of explanation that opposed that found in Christ. The fact is often overlooked that legalism and covetousness are two sides of the same deadly coin. They are both consequences of failing to recognize that the correct pattern of teaching is that laid down by the Lord and seen in Paul and the other apostles. The careful student of the word will observe that the apostles were as vigorously against materialism as they were against legalism. The man who has been taught the truth of God's grace stands in grave danger of succumbing to materialism. It would appear that the instructions on legalism are the "classroom" while we really test our understanding or write the exam by our slant on materialism. You can tell your understanding of God's grace by watching your stance on materialism.

The apostles consistently link false doctrine, covetousness and the love of self.

The commandments of men

13. This witness is true. Wherefore rebuke them sharply, that they may be sound in the faith; 14. Not giving heed to Jewish fables, and commandments of men, that turn from the truth.
Titus 1:13 - 14

Genesis to Malachi when properly taught would be teaching faith and love. Jewish fables is a reference to the sermons taught from the holy scriptures by men whose conclusion is a departure from the faith. Our faith is how Christ has explained the bible. Departing from the faith is departing from those things which Christ has taught. This is departure from sound doctrine. The minister who does not follow the mode of interpretation found in Christ teaches the explanation or doctrine of men!

The man that enters into the ministry of the word has enlisted in an age-old war over the souls of men. The contention is over how to correctly interpret and explain Genesis to Malachi.

Don't become frustrated

Always be eager to present yourself before God as a perfect and mature minister, without shame, as one who correctly explains the Word of Truth
2 Timothy 2:15 (TPT)

The margin of The Passion Translation reads "don't become frustrated." It also gives an alternate rendering, "Consider it a serious matter and keep on considering it something serious to present yourself before God."

We study to show ourselves approved so as to distinguish ourselves from others whose interpretation of Genesis to Malachi shows that they have turned from the truth.

16 as also in all his epistles, speaking in them of these things; in which are some things hard to be understood, which they that are unlearned and unstable wrest, as they do also the other Scriptures, unto their own destruction. 17 Ye therefore, beloved, seeing ye know these things before, beware lest ye also, being led away with the error of the wicked, fall from your own steadfastness.
2 Peter 3:16-17

The wisdom that Paul was given by God, which he used to explain the scriptures is the interpretation seen in Christ. Those that were unlearned and unstable found some of Paul's explanations hard to be understood.

Moses and the prophets had taught the message of the riches of salvation in the ancient texts of scripture in such dark, parabolic speech that the wicked or unbelieving used it to practice ordinances devoid of faith. Paul followed the wisdom of Christ and correctly explained those texts as converging on Christ. The error of the wicked was their refusal to accept that explanation. It was hard for them to understand that the ordinances were to teach faith and not ordinances. In unbelief they wouldn't accept Paul's testimony. Rather than accept Paul's mode of explanation, those who teach the Genesis to Malachi text as ordinances chose to remain in unbelief.

Peter shows that the problem was not with Paul. Paul had correctly handled the holy scriptures. Some people just found it hard to let go of modes of interpretation that had veiled the fact that God desired mercy and not sacrifice.

Peter instructs the saints not to be "led away with the error of the wicked".

What was Peter's solution?

18 But grow in grace, and in the knowledge of our Lord and Saviour Jesus Christ. To him be glory both now and for ever. Amen.
2 Peter 3:18

Rather than interpret scriptures in ways that oppose the revelation of Christ, grow in grace. Grace sees the scriptures as the knowledge of our Lord and Saviour Jesus Christ. In other words, don't be one of those who open Genesis to Malachi and teach it to others in a way that opposes the way that Jesus taught it and as Paul taught it.

10

What Jesus said about wealth

16. And without controversy great is the mystery of godliness: God was manifest in the flesh, justified in the Spirit, seen of angels, preached unto the Gentiles, believed on in the world, received up into glory.
1 Timothy 3:16

Without controversy means "without dissent" or "by consent of all". The agreed doctrine amongst the saints is that it was in the incarnation and work of Christ that men in particular and angels in addition, received great light about godliness or what God is like. Prior to Jesus manifesting in the flesh, God's character had been a mystery. It is understanding the humanity of Christ that we see the unexplained things of God made clear. The cobwebs in our thinking are removed so we see God clearly.

Jesus is God's hermeneutics.

16. For I am not ashamed of the gospel of Christ: for it is the power of God unto salvation to every one that believeth; to the Jew first, and also to the Greek.
Romans 1:16

In the cross of Christ, we see how God responds when attacked by men. God used His ability to absorb the violence that men measured out to Him. Rather than kill those who attacked Him, He died the death of man's sins. The challenge with this central revelation of the scriptures is that the Pharisees had already explained the large volume of sacred texts containing the killing of opposing armies in battle as descriptive of God's power. The gospel describes God's power as the riches of His kindness and mercy which caused Him to give up Himself in our place, dying for our sins and then rising from the dead on the third day. Thus, the power of God appears to be powerlessness to the unbelieving mind that wants that power to kill human enemies.

We have seen His glory

14. And the Word was made flesh, and dwelt among us, (and we beheld his glory, the glory as of the only begotten of the Father,) full of grace and truth.
John 1:14

John declared that in seeing Jesus in a flesh, blood and bone body we were witnessing the majesty and glory of God. When God finally showed up in man's world in His glory, we don't see the usual trappings of wealth.

Peter says we "were eyewitnesses of his majesty" (see 2 Peter 1:16). He meant that in observing Jesus he had observed the majesty of God. Jesus who looked so ordinary, who could be arrested by man and sentenced to death, who was not flashy and dazzling, who showed up without material pomp and blinding light was the majesty of God?

That majesty couldn't refer to miraculous power for while it is true that Jesus walked on water, Moses did not walk on water. He parted it and took a whole nation through the Red Sea without losing any. While it is true that Jesus fed 5000 men by multiplying loaves, Moses supplied Manna for a whole nation on a daily basis for 40 years. Yet, Moses is not the majesty and glory of God - Jesus is! God's glory fully displayed in Christ did not carry echoes of wealth and splendor. The majesty of God asked to be baptized by John, received sinners, suffered the humiliation of man and was the embodiment of the compassion and longsuffering of God.

That is God's glory and majesty.

The Lord Jesus clarified God's part in material wealth.

Jesus, not an expert on wealth creation

13. And one of the company said unto him, Master, speak to my brother, that he divide the inheritance with me. 14. And he said unto him, Man, who made me a judge or a divider over you? 15. And he said unto them, Take heed, and beware of covetousness: for a man's life consisteth not in the abundance of the things which he possesseth.

Luke 12:13 - 15

People offered Jesus the opportunity to lay down the "law" for wealth distribution because they assumed that was what ministers of the scriptures do.

Jesus' response to this request was, "Man, who made me a judge or a divider over you?" Jesus' response shows that He did not recognize that God had made Him a judge on such matters. The mandate to teach or preach the gospel did not confer such powers. Jesus openly admitted that someone needed to give him the rights. Jesus meant that such roles were man-made and that as a minister of the gospel, He was not authoritative on material wealth division. The minister preaches the gospel as God's way of giving the riches of salvation. His message is not the acquisition or distribution of material wealth. Although the rich invited Him to teach on wealth distribution, Jesus didn't function as a minister of wealth distribution.

Jesus preached the riches of contentment. "He said unto them, Take heed, and beware of covetousness". "Beware of covetousness" is not standard counsel to the one who feels he is about to be cheated out of his inheritance. However, that is the gospel.

His answer shows that He recognized that there were men who already knew about how the financial system and material wealth worked on earth. Rather than teach about how to divide the wealth, He taught about our attitudes towards the material resources already acquired. Jesus taught about the motives and use of wealth and not how to obtain it. He did not say anything about how the inheritance should be distributed.

In this, Jesus ministered the explanation of the Father's nature. If the distribution and acquisition was of God the Lord Jesus would have explained it. The distribution of money does not reveal God. The distribution of money is in man's power. Both saints and sinners have material wealth. Both saints and sinners are also poor.

Covetousness would refer to the control that the riches of this world exercises over those who trust in it. Material riches make a poor master but an excellent servant.

Here's the full text of Jesus' response:

Take heed, and beware of covetousness: for a man's life consisteth not in the abundance of the things which he possesseth (see Luke 12:15).

Jesus taught that man's life consists not in ownership but in giving. It is a surprising fact that the gospel doesn't major on ownership. The gospel gives instruction about generosity.

Then, He gave a parable to teach the same truth:

Jesus' parable on the measurement of wealth

16. And he spake a parable unto them, saying, The ground of a certain rich man brought forth plentifully: 17. And he thought within himself, saying, What shall I do, because I have no room where to bestow my fruits? 18. And he said, This will I do: I will pull down my barns, and build greater; and there will I bestow all my fruits and my goods. 19. And I will say to my soul, Soul, thou hast much goods laid up for many years; take thine ease, eat, drink, and be merry. 20. But God said unto him, Thou fool, this night thy soul shall be required of thee: then whose shall those things be, which thou hast provided? 21. So is he that layeth up treasure for himself, and is not rich toward God.

Luke 12:16 – 21

Jesus said, “the ground of a rich man” – this agrees with the fact that God has given the earth to men. Jesus does not say, “the ground of a spiritual man”.

“A certain rich man whose ground brought forth plentifully” means that it is the men that own the ground that influence the direction of financial flow on the earth. Men have a lot more to do with the flow of material wealth on the earth than religious people are willing to admit.

Jesus’ statement, “then whose shall those things be, which thou hast provided?” gives food for thought. He doesn’t describe the abundance as that which God personally gave that rich man. Although we like to use that term, Jesus did not say that the man’s wealth was divine favour. He simply stated that the abundance was the rich man’s possession. This agrees with his statement “A man’s life consists not in the abundance of the things which he possessed”. He spoke of wealth as a function of human activity (how the rich man used his ground).

The man’s material wealth was not a mysterious factor – it was linked to the abundance of his ground.

Jesus does not say the man forfeited getting more wealth because he failed to give. Although the man wasn’t a giver, his investments yielded maximum profit. His ground brought forth plentifully. It was such a significant increase that the man said, “I have no room where to bestow my fruits”. Jesus separates a man’s giving and spirituality from his ability to receive material wealth through enterprise.

The story of the rich fool shows that building a capacity for wealth is given to men independent of their spirituality. Although this man had not prioritized spiritual things and was not a giver, Jesus acknowledges that he accumulated significant material riches.

This rich man already knew how to get wealth through enterprise. Although the rich man was a fool, he was not intellectually dull or lacking in business savviness. He lacked gospel sense. He likely lived in a system that was encouraging of industry and he understood how to increase his financial portfolio. Yet, Jesus refers to the rich man as a fool. The man was a fool because his life consisted in wealth accumulation. He did not recognize God's riches which affects how a man uses his material wealth to bless.

In this intriguing parable, God asks, "Thou fool, this night thy soul shall be required of thee: then whose shall those things be, which thou hast provided?"

Some would say that the rich fool had laid up his wealth for a righteous man to acquire. The truth is that Jesus did not say that the rich man had acquired his wealth as a result of a wealth transfer from another sinner. His parable shows that the man's wealth was a product of industry. Since Jesus said nothing about wealth transfer, but stated a question, "then whose shall those things be, which thou hast provided?" – we should do the same.

Many would not stop where Jesus stopped. There is a grave danger in not leaving His question as a question.

That expression "rich toward God" means that the wealth that the gospel teaches about is measured not by the rate at which man can build up a fortune but by how man distributes it to meet the need of others. It is this gospel-wealth that Jesus taught about. Thus, the materially rich man was poor towards God or poor in gospel terms. Stated more concisely, Jesus and the apostles did not teach give-to-get but now-that-you-have-give.

Jesus is showing that the factors responsible for building financial power are not spiritual in nature. He did not teach material riches as a reward for spirituality. Also, Jesus did not see the material wealth as a barrier. Jesus' teaching was that although the man had acquired significant material wealth through enterprise, the man was not rich toward God!

The gospel does not measure ownership but giving to express the true riches of God. The Lord measured God's riches not in the getting of the material wealth but in the use and distribution of it for God's glory.

The rich fool measured wealth as one who was covetous. He was not called a fool because he was materially rich but because he wasn't rich towards God. Although the man was business savvy, he was lacking in expressing the true wealth of being a blessing to others. Jesus' teaching focused on destroying the grip of covetousness by expressing the riches of generosity. This is one big reason for giving.

The abundance of money is not a vice nor does Jesus describe it as evil. The evil is covetousness. It is the heart trusting in material wealth that is referred to as covetousness. The gospel establishes that the heart of man must not be controlled by the possessions.

Men like the rich fool already knew how to acquire wealth. As a gospel minister, Jesus was big on being rich towards God. This is the riches of liberality. Jesus' explanation challenges our worldview by classifying a man who is only rich in this world but not rich towards God as poor. A business-savvy man builds up tremendous wealth, while the gospel savvy man knows how to give it to bless others. Jesus majored on the riches of giving. The Lord Jesus did not focus as much on the man's trade as He focused on generosity.

It is somewhat mind-boggling that while it is true that He spoke a lot about money, He did not teach His hearers how to get rich.

In reality, in the gospel accounts, all those described as rich were already rich before they met Jesus as He went about His ministry. Jesus did not teach that they needed to come in contact with His ministry in order to become materially wealthy.

Jesus was not sent to teach how to acquire wealth.

A careful study of the scriptures shows that Jesus' impact on those that He encountered was not that they became materially richer as a result of their interactions with Him. Instead, when they believed His message, they recognized the riches of generosity.

Jesus taught along similar lines in His rebuke of the Pharisees:

9. And I say unto you, Make to yourselves friends of the mammon of unrighteousness; that, when ye fail, they may receive you into everlasting habitations. 10. He that is faithful in that which is least is faithful also in much: and he that is unjust in the least is unjust also in much. 11. If therefore ye have not been faithful in the unrighteous mammon, who will commit to your trust the true riches?

Luke 16:9 - 11

We can decipher Jesus' teaching by the effect of these words on the Pharisees who heard Him.

And the Pharisees also, who were covetous, heard all these things: and they derided him (see Luke 16: 14). They rejected what Jesus taught in relation to God's riches. They saw material riches as validation of spirituality. The Pharisees understood that Jesus was teaching about covetousness.

Jesus taught about being faithful in that which is least. He referred to the riches of this world as "that which is least." This means that the "mammon of unrighteousness" was not true riches.

The Pharisees had misplaced their trust. They had acquired "unrighteous mammon" but had not been faithful in their use of it. This misplaced trust in the riches of this world is referred to as covetousness. The covetousness of the Pharisees blinded them to true riches. True riches is referred to as being rich towards God. It is measured by liberty and freedom in giving.

Jesus consistently specialized in teaching about the motives and use of wealth and not how to obtain it – these Pharisees already knew how to obtain wealth. Jesus' teaching showed that the Pharisees' covetousness meant that they were lacking the true wealth of being a blessing to others. The Pharisees' unbelief meant that they rejected the ability inherent in Jesus' teaching to destroy the grip of covetousness. They resisted the riches of generosity.

In His earthly ministry, Jesus severally acknowledged faith for healing.

It Is noteworthy that no gospel writer ever presented Him saying to anyone, "your faith has made you materially wealthy." Jesus does not associate faith with the amassing of wealth. Men have successfully amassed considerable wealth independent of faith in Jesus. The faith or faithfulness that Jesus consistently associates with riches is the true riches of giving to bless others.

Was Jesus clueless about wealth acquisition?

From the teachings of the Lord Jesus, He shows a healthy grasp of the workings of wealth in the natural world.

Although the Lord does not focus on how the rich fool made his money, we can infer from the pulling down of barns that the Lord knew that making room for more capacity is a sound business principle.

2. And the Pharisees and scribes murmured, saying, This man receiveth sinners, and eateth with them. 3. And he spake this parble unto them, saying, 4. What man of you, having an hundred sheep, if he lose one of them, doth not leave the ninety and nine in the wilderness, and go after that which is lost, until he find it? 5. And when he hath found it, he layeth it on his shoulders, rejoicing.

Luke 15:2 - 5

The Lord was teaching the Pharisees and scribes about the effect of man's repentance when the gospel is preached. He was not teaching business principles. Although Jesus' parables are about God's method of salvation in the kingdom, it is easy to see that He recognizes how good business is run. He knew how business men labour to recover business losses.

The "man" in "which man of you, having an hundred sheep" is a business man trading in sheep. Jesus recognized that the good business man does not have slumped shoulders over business losses but locates and recovers that which was lost.

Jesus used the big professions of His day to illustrate how men acquired material wealth by the diligent application of labour in the market place. Jesus' examples do not portray a priest, prophet or preacher of the gospel increasing in material wealth in the discharge of their duty.

A house of prayer

13. And the Jews' passover was at hand, and Jesus went up to Jerusalem, 14. And found in the temple those that sold oxen and sheep and doves, and the changers of money sitting: 15. And when he had made a scourge of small cords, he drove them all out of the temple, and the sheep, and the oxen; and poured out the changers' money, and overthrew the tables; 16. And said unto them that sold doves, Take these things hence; make not my Father's house an house of merchandise.

John 2: 13 - 16

The Psalmist says, "thou desirest not sacrifice; else would I give it: thou delightest not in burnt offering" (see Psalm 51: 16, Hebrews 10:6). The "them all" that Jesus drove out of the temple were the sheep and oxen that were being used for temple sacrifice in a system that God had not even requested to start with. The sacrifices were to be a teaching aid that Jesus would be the sacrifice for sins. The doctrine of the Pharisees revered the sheep and the oxen without understanding that which they stood for. Some people had even started a money exchange business right within the temple. Scholars said it was in the area dedicated to the gentiles. The God-given job of preaching the gospel for salvation had been replaced with the man-made job of using the temple for wealth-acquisition. In that system, the minister preaches the acquisition of wealth. Thus, covetousness had caused the Pharisees to close the door of salvation and opened the door of merchandise. Therefore, they sold oxen, sheep and doves in it. The fact that these money changers were sitting can only mean that business was booming. The doctrine of the Pharisees used good words and fair speeches to deceive the hearts of the simple, made merchandise of their hearers and turned the place of fellowship to the "house of merchandise!"

Jesus was not attacking industry. He was making the case that the temple was to be a house of prayer and not a business center. It is an important matter of distinction in function. Jesus preached a distinction between the local assembly and what He referred to as "the house of merchandise."

As a man or woman, the minister can be wealthy but it wouldn't be from preaching.

Paul taught that the house of God, which is the church of the living God is the ground and pillar of truth (see 1 Timothy 3:15). That truth is not just any truth but the ground of the truth of the gospel. Men that try to make the church the ground and pillar of financial education misunderstand the purpose and function of the local assembly.

11

Trust in the living God

Paul's teaching on the use of wealth is a clarification of the teachings of the holy scriptures.

What has the living God given us richly?

17. Charge them that are rich in this world, that they be not highminded, nor trust in uncertain riches, but in the living God, who giveth us richly all things to enjoy; 18. That they do good, that they be rich in good works, ready to distribute, willing to communicate;

1 Timothy 6:17 - 18

The fact that those saints "that are rich in this world" are to become "rich in good works" means that becoming materially rich is not the good works! The fact that the saints that are rich in this world are to be taught to be rich in good works means that one does not become materially rich by being rich in good works.

Paul is saying, "now that you are rich in this world, here are some instructions for you". Thus, he mentions being rich in this world as a starting point and not a destination.

Who are the "them that are rich in this world"?

Paul wrote the Roman Epistle "to all that be in Rome, beloved of God, called to be saints" (see Romans 1:7)

Paul wrote the Corinthian Epistle "Unto the church of God which is at Corinth, to them that are sanctified in Christ Jesus, called to be saints" (see 1 Corinthians 1:2)

Paul wrote the Galatian Epistle "unto the churches of Galatia (see Galatians 1:2)

Paul wrote the Ephesian Epistle "to the saints which are at Ephesus, and to the faithful in Christ Jesus" (see Ephesians 1:1)

Thus, the epistles are not written for the church to govern the world by but for the spiritual growth of the saints. Therefore, in his instructions to Timothy, Paul is teaching Timothy in order that Timothy might teach the saints.

Timothy's audience are saints.

The Greek word translated "world" in "rich in this world" conveys the idea of interactions and activity amongst men on earth. To be rich in this world gives us a clue as to the source of their riches. It tells us that they acquired their material wealth by building and leveraging associations with other human beings in commercial interactions. These activities might have been in money-lending, commanding military forces, kings living by the taxes levied on their subjects or they may even have been obtained by operating as leaders of industry. Paul doesn't tell us the specific interactions.

Since we already established that the epistles are written to saints, "them that are rich in this world" would refer to those saints in Timothy's audience who had become financially and materially wealthy by leveraging social and commercial workings on the earth.

"Charge them that are rich in this world" is not addressed to the sinner. Paul is telling Timothy to charge those saints that have material abundance.

Paul's "charge them that are rich in this world" means that amongst the saints there were those who were rich in this world and those who were not rich in this world. Paul doesn't promise the saints that they would all be rich in this world nor does he dwell on it – as a matter of fact, not all saints would be rich in this world. There are many factors responsible for this. People's financial standing is independent of their spiritual maturity or lack of. Since some saints are rich in this world while others are poor it would mean that neither poverty nor money are God's gifts in redemption. Both money and poverty are products of human interaction, are man-made and belong to humanity. Since money is man-made, it cannot be redeemed by God. It belongs in the sphere of man.

The saints who were rich were not said to be super-saints on account of their material wealth, neither were the poorer saints labelled inferior or lacking in spirituality or failing to "possess their possessions". The absence or presence of money was not the hallmark of spirituality in the Epistles.

These saints who are "rich in this world" had become materially well-off by the way that they had engaged in the affairs of this earth. Paul does not major on the specifics of what they did in order to be wealthy. He did not recommend a particular trade as the Christian trade. This should make sense because there is no currency called "Christian money". Rather than confer holiness on particular jobs and make them appear more spiritual than others, the apostle concerns himself with their disposition towards riches acquired through enterprise. His charge was "not to trust". Paul did not say that the saints were not to make money. He said they were not to trust in their financial clout or the lack of it.

Two riches contrasted

17. Charge them that are rich in this world, that they be not highminded, nor trust in uncertain riches, but in the living God, who giveth us richly all things to

enjoy; 18. That they do good, that they be rich in good works, ready to distribute, willing to communicate;
1 Timothy 6:17 - 18

Paul introduces two types of riches. He speaks of "rich in this world" and "rich in good works".

Paul's "rich in this world" refers to material wealth or "riches" by acquisition through interaction with market forces.

Paul calls having money being "rich in this world". He does not call it the riches of God. This gives us clues that the determination of who would be materially rich or not is not something that God controls.

Over and above being "rich in this world", Paul teaches "rich in good works", which from the context of its usage is a form of riches other than acquiring material possessions. "Rich in good works" is being "rich", not as acquisition but as distribution of that previously acquired. He doesn't just mention "rich in good works" like he had mentioned "rich in this world". He emphasizes "rich in good works" by explaining "rich in good works" in detail. The riches that Paul told Timothy to teach the saints was the riches of good works. The riches of good works is a gift of redemption. He referred to this as the riches of liberality when commending the Macedonians (see 2 Corinthians 8:2).

So we see that while "rich in this world" is material, of this world and earthy, "rich in good works" uses materials although it is not material in nature. The riches of good works are not of this world. Those riches are of the living God. They are spiritual.

Paul described "rich in this world" as riches not to be trusted in, for they are uncertain riches.

Now, we realize that the riches of redemption cannot be referred to as "uncertain riches". The word translated "rich" means "to supply". "Uncertain riches" imply that there are uncertain supplies. It would be improper to refer to God's supply in Christ as uncertain. Those riches or supplies that God supplied are what He has chosen that we measure His reputation by.

Paul's reference to material wealth as uncertain riches would mean that money is not a gift of redemption. Men already had tremendous material wealth before salvation was supplied in Christ. God's faithfulness is His fellowship "of his Son Jesus Christ our Lord" (see 1 Corinthians 1:9). Fellowship speaks of supply. Thus, God has staked His reputation on His supply of the riches of redemption by raising Jesus from the dead (see Hebrews 6:17-18, Acts 13:32-33). We measure His faithfulness in His supply of life by the resurrection of Jesus - this is sure "riches".

Although Paul qualified "rich in this world" as "uncertain riches", he does not teach that "rich in this world" is contrary to, antagonistic towards or opposed to "rich in good works". Paul instructed saints who already possessed the riches of salvation to use being "rich in this world" to express the riches of good works.

Since Timothy had to charge those saints who had become rich in this world to express the riches of good works, it means that those saints did not acquire their material riches through spirituality. Paul's instruction would mean that the saints who were materially rich do not acquire those riches by giving. More importantly, this clarifies that the riches of good works is not so the saint might qualify for being "rich in this world." Paul's instructions imply that both types of riches can be seen in the same saint.

To overcome being "high minded", saints are taught to trust or depend on God's invisible resources, which is His spirit given to us as His supply of riches in the New Birth. We pray for saints and train them through the word to continually draw their confidence from the riches of the spirit and not from uncertain riches.

The fellow who has material resources but doesn't share with others is not "rich in good works". To be "rich in good works" is to be rich towards God.

To be "rich in this world" is not evil. We do not trust in those riches for they are uncertain - they come and go. By referring to "rich in this world" as uncertain, he shows that there was nothing to be done to make it certain. The saint is to relate to it as uncertain.

The implication is that the riches of good works is certain. It endures. It is eternal in duration and quality for it is of God.

One of the chief lessons of redemption is the riches of good works in those that believe. Therefore, we teach the riches of good works as a truth of redemption.

It is noteworthy that it is the same Greek word that is used for "rich" in both "rich in this world" and "rich in good works". It is as we examine the usage of rich in both instances that we see that "rich" does not refer to the same thing although used by the same author to the same audience within the same chapter and just a few verses apart! We cannot afford to fix meanings to the word "rich".

Rather than trust in uncertain riches, the saint is to trust in "the living God".

Recognizing what God has supplied in Christ

9. God is faithful, by whom ye were called unto the fellowship of his Son Jesus Christ our Lord.
1 Corinthians 1:9

The word translated "fellowship" in the KJV describes God reaching out to us. Fellowship means supply. It refers to God's gift. Thus, fellowship in relation to God is not something you initiate. It is your response to that which He has initiated.

Fellowship means that we receive what He has given. That is fellowship between man and God.

The fellowship of His son describes what God supplied, gave or made available in His Son.

The gospel that saved us was that we believed in our heart that God had raised Jesus from the dead (see Romans 10:8-11). Thus, what God supplied is the resurrection. God's promised blessing or riches was that "we might receive the promise of the Spirit through faith" (see Galatians 3:14).

15. And for this cause he is the mediator of the new testament, that by means of death, for the redemption of the transgressions that were under the first testament, they which are called might receive the promise of eternal inheritance.
Hebrews 9:15

"They which are called" are called through the gospel, which proclaims what God has done in Christ. All respond to God's call of salvation by believing the gospel. This is how we receive the promise of eternal inheritance. The promise is now fulfilled. It is no longer a promise. It is our possession in Christ.

God has fulfilled His promise of eternal inheritance by His supply through the sacrifice of Christ.

Since the promise is intrinsically eternal, it cannot refer to material things which by definition perish (see 1 Peter 1:18). Houses, cars, shoes and clothes are necessary human needs but they are not God's inheritance received by believing the gospel. This eternal inheritance is the eternal spirit that we received at the instant we answered His call by believing the gospel. By believing the gospel, we have received His spirit which He Has given to us.

But Christ, because he lives for ever, possesses a priesthood that needs no successor. This means that he can save fully and completely those who approach God through him, for he is always living to intercede on their behalf.
Hebrews 7: 25 (PHILLIPS)

The J.B. Phillips translation affirms Jesus' ability to "save fully and completely". This means that when Jesus saves, He saves completely. He is not planning to complete this. It is complete. He has done it. It is done.

Therefore, He is able also to save forever (completely, perfectly, for eternity) those who come to God through Him, since He always lives to intercede and intervene on their behalf [with God].
Hebrews 7: 25 (AMP)

Jesus is the man that continues for ever. The J.B. Phillips translation translates that as Jesus possessing "a priesthood that needs no successor".

This truth that "He ever liveth" is key. The fact that He continues ever without the possibility of there ever being a successor means that He has an unchangeable priesthood that guarantees the safety of that committed to His priesthood.

He guarantees that our spirit is perfected forever.

We trust in the living God or demonstrate our confidence in the fact of His eternal inheritance in us by depending on His spirit in us.

14. The grace of the Lord Jesus Christ, and the love of God, and the communion of the Holy Ghost, be with you all. Amen.
2 Corinthians 13: 14

That word translated communion is the word usually translated fellowship. It means "to supply". The grace of our Lord Jesus is the love of God seen in the fact of resurrection. God's love gave us the spirit, which we receive in the New Birth. Thus, the spirit is the father's supply. To trust in the living God is to trust in the spirit as His riches in us.

Paul based his appeal to the Galatians on this fact of their reception of God's supply of the spirit. He said, "this only would I learn of you, received ye the Spirit by the works of the law, or by the hearing of faith?" (see Galatians 3:2). The hearing of faith means the news of God's works, which is His supply of the spirit in the resurrection of Jesus. (see also Galatians 3:14)

His spirit which we received of Him is His riches given to us to enjoy. In the context of Paul's letter to Timothy, by His spirit as His riches in us, God has given us the riches of good works to enjoy.

Our subjection unto the gospel

In line with what he taught Timothy, this is how Paul taught the Corinthians to "trust in the living God":

13. Whiles by the experiment of this ministration they glorify God for your professed subjection unto the gospel of Christ, and for your liberal distribution unto them, and unto all men;
2 Corinthians 9:13

Liberal distribution is giving. Paul is encouraging the saints at Corinth to respond to God's seed in them by supplying material support to others ("them" referred to the saints in Jerusalem who were going through hard times).

"This ministration" is the riches of "liberal distribution" by the Corinthians. Paul wasn't describing how to be a nice saint. He was teaching "professed subjection unto the gospel of Christ". The gospel of Christ is the grace that resulted in Jesus giving Himself sacrificially so that we might receive the riches of righteousness. This is the message of God's fellowship - His distribution to us is Christ in us as riches.

"Subjection to the gospel of Christ" is the knowledge of God's distribution towards us in Christ causing us to distribute to others liberally or lavishly for we have His spirit. This is God's example seen clearly in Christ.

Thus, to "trust in the living God" is to respond to the supply of His spirit in us by being, "ready to distribute and willing to communicate." We show that trust by acting on the riches of good works, which is the riches of liberality or the sacrifice of praise. It is contentment.

God has given us richly all those things that we have seen in Christ as true riches. Our enjoyment is to trust His riches in us by showing forth the riches of good works.

God has given the earth to all men irrespective of their beliefs and race. However, it is to the saint that He has given the riches of liberality to enjoy.

In context, the high-minded saints are those who assume that uncertain riches are God's gift in Christ, whereas the gospel teaches the riches of liberality as God's gift to His saints. The riches offered by the living God are not the uncertain riches of this earth. Timothy was to combat this high-mindedness by teaching the riches of good works as God's riches given to His saints. The saint has received eternal life as God's heredity in His saints. Eternal life then manifests as the riches of good works in the saint.

What is Timothy's charge?

Paul explained "God has given us richly all things to enjoy" as "they do good, that they be rich in good works, ready to distribute, willing to communicate". In receiving Christ as God's gift, we received the ability to give as God gives. This ability to give as God gives because of His heredity in us is the "all things" in "God who giveth us richly all things to enjoy". The riches of good works means that we give to others as Christ gave Himself for us in redemption. We teach these facts of the gospel to those who have already accepted its message for salvation so that they would understand that within that salvation is the ability to share with others.

The expression, "to trust in the living God" means that the saint is not to ignore the nature of God, which is the inheritance of all saints in the New Birth. The saint is to yield to that nature and be governed by it. The willingness to distribute is embedded in the nature of God that we have received. We obey the nature of love in us because obedience is an end in itself and not a means to an end. Paul instructs Timothy to teach the truth of it to the saints so they can acknowledge this fact of the riches of good works.

Although, the living God has given His saints the riches of good works, the saint can embrace covetousness and become blinded to God's ability or ignore it through lack of sound teaching. The commandments of men, which is a departure from the doctrine of Christ appeals to the flesh and results in making covetousness acceptable.

To trust in the living God would mean renewing the mind to the fact that we do not share with others in order to get ahead financially. When we share, we are acknowledging the Father's nature. For the saints, sharing with others is an end in itself.

The nature of God, which He has given to us in the new creation, is rich in good works, ready to distribute and willing to communicate. Teaching saints to find their wealth (the riches of good works) in the sharing of the "riches of this world" with others is a teaching of redemption. This God-given ability to give with the freedom with which God gives is the "all things" that are variously described as doing good, being rich in good works, ready to distribute and willing to communicate. It is the exceeding greatness of God's power at work through the saint.

We can say it a little differently to drive home the point:

The Epistles teach the saints to trust in riches. These would be those riches of salvation, which is the riches of liberality that God lavishly gave to us through the gospel.

Through the gospel, Paul teaches the saint not to trust in riches. These would be the riches that are acquired as a result of interactions in the natural world.

We observe that Paul doesn't tell Timothy to charge the saints about how to be rich in this world. There is nothing wrong with saints having the riches of this world. However, teaching saints how to make money or acquire more of the riches of this world is not the scope of the gospel – there are places for learning such needful things.

I am rich, and increased with goods

There is danger in seeing money as a gift of Christ's sacrifice. It should be obvious that money is not supplied in the finished work of Christ for money predated the coming of Christ, it was used while He was on earth, and is still being used after His resurrection. While money is independent of Christ's sacrifice, our disposition towards money is a gift of redemption.

We remember John's stern rebuke of the saints at Laodicea:

17. Because thou sayest, I am rich, and increased with goods, and have need of nothing; and knowest not that thou art wretched, and miserable, and poor, and blind, and naked:
Revelation 3:17

There is absolutely nothing wrong with having lots of money.

A casual reading would make it look like John held it against them that they were rich and had increased their investment portfolio. However, John pointed out that the trouble at Laodicea had to do with their "saying". That saying refers to their doctrine. They preached a corruption of the true gospel that measured wealth by increase in material acquisition. This is departure from the doctrine of Christ. This means that John's rebuke of the Laodiceans is directed at the teaching ministries in their midst. These ministers celebrated the acquisition of material possessions. Their doctrine resulted in the saints trusting in uncertain riches. They had looked away from the true riches of liberality towards covetousness. The Lord describes that doctrine as wretchedness. Paul warned about such ministries and doctrines "Now I beseech you, brethren, mark them which cause divisions and offences contrary to the doctrine which ye have learned; and avoid them. For they that are such serve not our Lord Jesus Christ, but their own belly; and by good words and fair speeches deceive the hearts of the simple" (see Romans 16: 17 – 18). The use of good sounding words and fair speeches to deceive the saints explains the Laodicean challenge. A minister that focuses the gospel on the acquisition of the riches of this world is not training the saints in the riches of kindness and service of the Lord by serving His saints. It stirs up selfishness. They are serving their own belly

The Laodicean doctrine had a misplaced emphasis. They should have responded to God's love by loving the brethren with the riches of God's love. They gloried in acquisition of material wealth when the riches of good works would rejoice in the joy of sharing with others.

To saints with such a confession "I am rich, and increased with goods", the rebuke of John was "and knowest not that thou art wretched, and miserable, and poor, and blind, and naked". John assured the saints in Laodicea who were materially wealthy, and had increased with goods to the point where they had need of nothing that they were poor! He meant that they were poor in the riches of good works.

Thus, the teaching of the epistles is that the saint who has the riches of this world, but who is not also rich in good works is poor in gospel terms. It is high-mindedness to use the acquisition of material riches or the increase of such to measure a man's faith. Faith with respect to material riches is seen in the riches of good works, which is the riches of liberality.

We are grateful and thankful for the opportunities that we get in this life. Gratitude is good and is to be encouraged. However, we cross over into dangerous territory when we treat the possession of uncertain riches as proof of God's favour. When we start measuring God's favour by the absence or presence of lack, we are under the grip of covetousness. By definition, uncertain riches fluctuate. One doesn't need the gospel in order to have those riches. They come in cycles of scarcity as well as periods of abundance. The riches that the epistles major on are not measured by the material supplies one has or doesn't have.

Timothy was to teach giving, not wealth acquisition

Paul's "charge them that are rich in this world" would mean that Paul did not consider Timothy as one of the materially rich ones. Paul couldn't in good conscience tell Timothy to be authoritative on how to acquire material wealth when Timothy might not be rich in this world. Even if Timothy was rich in this world, Paul was writing to Timothy as a Man of God and not as a business man – there is a difference. Paul's instructions to Timothy show that the gospel concerns itself with distributing and communicating the material wealth already possessed. As a minister of the gospel, it is the riches of good works that Timothy is to be expert with. The gospel teaches the business man to be a minister – to show forth the praises of Him by offering spiritual sacrifices continually. The gospel does not teach the business man the secrets for getting more business.

Timothy's charge was to encourage the saints who already knew how to engage and galvanize the riches of the earth to give themselves over to ministry. They were not engaging in the ministry to get the riches of this world. This ministry is their testimony of the example seen in Christ. It is not the acquisition of wealth. The acquisition of wealth is business and enterprise. Ministry is first giving yourself to the Lord and then unto others.

Paul taught the difference between business and ministry to the Ephesians:

28. Let him that stole steal no more: but rather let him labour, working with his hands the thing which is good, that he may have to give to him that needeth.
Ephesians 4:28

The saint reading this in Ephesus was already aware of the riches of grace, the riches of mercy and Christ as the riches of a recreated spirit in the first three chapters of Ephesians. Paul then addresses poor conduct in the saint who has God's riches. Paul's teaching was that such should work so they have what they need and surplus to give to others who are in need. Although, it is implied that one might get wealthy by having a good job, Paul does not major on that in his teaching. Paul isn't teaching how to get wealthy, he is teaching "steal no more … labour … give" – this is honest living. Paul does not teach the saint that money is one of the riches in Christ. He teaches this

saint the riches of working with one's hands. A saint who knows the gospel would work a job.
Paul does not go into details about particular jobs to do.

Why does Paul not go into details?

Although Paul was a business man, he did not write as a business man but as one entrusted with the gospel. Paul said, "I continue unto this day, witnessing both to small and great, saying none other things than those which the prophets and Moses did say should come" (see Acts 26:22). Paul witnessed "both to small and great" means that the social status of our hearers doesn't change the contents of the gospel that we preach. Paul's job was to preach the same gospel to both! Teaching saints how to make money or acquire more of the riches of this world is not the scope of the gospel.

Paul's "that he may have to give to him that needeth" isn't teaching how to turn the church into the house of merchandise. He is teaching the man in Christ to put the riches of God to work by meeting needs with his material resources. Ministering material things to others as a consequence of God's love in you is a strong message of redemption. Since it is ministry, those material things I distribute and communicate towards you leave my life and come into yours to enrich you. It is my ministry to you. It is spiritual sacrifice. Ministering to you is not in order that I may reap material benefits from my giving (that's investment really). If I give to you as a "soil" for reaping harvests for myself, I have succeeded in deceiving myself into ministering to myself. Giving as an expression of the riches of liberality or the riches of good works is offering up the sacrifice of praise.

Considering Paul's other writings, we see that the saint distributes and communicates to his own household, to those ministries that bless him or her spiritually and to the local assembly. Since Paul taught Timothy that the bible is uniquely authoritative on redemption, and Paul consistently gave clear teaching about the use of material wealth, it means that the correct use of material wealth is a teaching of redemption.

There is nothing stopping those saints who have the riches of this world from teaching Timothy the basics of how to be rich in this world while Timothy taught them the riches of good works. Many ministers of the gospel would save themselves from needless trouble concerning finances if they would learn from those saints who have the riches of this world.

12

Give and it shall be given unto you

38. Give, and it shall be given unto you; good measure, pressed down, and shaken together, and running over, shall men give into your bosom. For with the same measure that ye mete withal it shall be measured to you again.
Luke 6:38

We have taught all sorts from this text:

If you want to receive healing from God "pressed down shaken together and overflowing", go lay hands on the sick.

If you want to have your material needs met by God "pressed down shaken together and overflowing", go give to ministries who are "fertile" ground or better still, give to the rich.

Notice the emphasis on "If you want"?

In the circles that I grew up in, this text has a mantra that goes like this …. "offering time is blessing time".

Is this so?

Immediate context shows that Jesus is not dealing with finances specifically. He discusses judgement, condemnation and forgiveness of sins as it is practiced amongst men and by extension how God does not practice the forgiveness of sins!

Who does the giving in "it shall be given" unto you?

The text says, "shall men give into your bosom." Thus, Jesus does not place God in Luke 6:38. It is men that do the giving in "it shall be given" unto you.

Luke 6:38 describes how men give or reciprocate amongst one another. It is a fact that man would equally reciprocate a good turn as they would a bad turn. It is also a close approximation of the way the law operates.

The text does not teach that God gives to us because we gave to Him or that our act of giving makes Him owe us. Jesus is describing the system that govern human interactions on the earth.

20 And he lifted up his eyes on his disciples, and said, Blessed be ye poor: for yours is the kingdom of God.
Luke 6:20

3 Blessed are the poor in spirit: for theirs is the kingdom of heaven.
Matthew 5:3

The wordings of Luke 6:20 corresponds to Matthew 5:3, which is the sermon on the mount, therefore we see that Jesus is teaching the same thing in both places. In Matthew 5, Jesus explains the word of faith, which shows the love of God. He also explains how the hard-hearted man, who doesn't believe in God's mercy would act. We must know when we read of God's characteristics and when we are reading of the hardness of man's heart. The passage in Luke 6 is Luke's equivalent of Matthew 5. It is the sermon on the mount couched in Lucan language.

Matthew 5 sheds light on Luke 6.

1 Judge not, that ye be not judged. 2 For with what judgment ye judge, ye shall be judged: and with what measure ye mete, it shall be measured to you again.
Matthew 7:1-2

37 Judge not, and ye shall not be judged: condemn not, and ye shall not be condemned: forgive, and ye shall be forgiven: 38 give, and it shall be given unto you; good measure, pressed down, and shaken together, and running over, shall men give into your bosom. For with the same measure that ye mete withal it shall be measured to you again.
Luke 6:37-38

The passage in Matthew 7:1-2 is the same as Luke 6:37-38.

Matthew 7:2 documents how hard-hearted men, who don't believe in God's mercy operate tit for tat or reciprocals (you scratch my back and I scratch yours ideology). Thus, Luke 6:38 is the way of unbelief. Jesus is highlighting how hard-hearted men "give into your bosom" by responding to venom with venom. Based on both the Matthew 7 passage and Luke 6:37, we know what is given in Luke 6:38. Men, who have rejected God's mercy are judging each other by withholding mercy from each other. One man's fury triggers the same operation of the flesh in others who will escalate matters and withhold mercy from one another in their dealings.

Therefore, we know for a fact that Luke 6:38 is Jesus' explaining the ways of men who do not operate the riches of mercy. The concept is rephrased in Hebrews as "every transgression and disobedience received a just recompense of reward" (see Hebrews 2:2). The system of recompensing faults is not God's system. The Law is made for men who do not believe the gospel. Jesus was giving those Jews who were under the Law some insight about the law of sin and death. It is how men who do not obey the law of love operate. They do not see God as merciful, therefore they are not merciful.

God gives without finding fault

5 If any of you lack wisdom, let him ask of God, that giveth to all men liberally, and upbraideth not; and it shall be given him.
James 1:5

God's giving is liberal, without defamation, accusation or fault finding. This means that God does not consider the recipient before giving. His giving is not predicated on the recipient doing something to qualify. He doesn't give as "payback".

James said later:

16 Do not err, my beloved brethren. 17 Every good gift and every perfect gift is from above, and cometh down from the Father of lights, with whom is no variableness, neither shadow of turning.
James 1:16-17

James explains God as one with whom is no variableness, which means that God doesn't change. He said this while explaining God as the giver of perfect gift. God doesn't change in His character of giving. It is error to say that God adopts different modes in His giving.

34 For he whom God hath sent speaketh the words of God: for God giveth not the Spirit by measure unto him.
John 3:34

We observe that "unto him" is italicized. It should read "God giveth not the Spirit by measure." This shows the character of God in giving. God does not give His spirit by measure because He is not that kind of giver who gives by measure.

45 that ye may be the children of your Father which is in heaven: for he maketh his sun to rise on the evil and on the good, and sendeth rain on the just and on the unjust.
Matthew 5:45

We know this is still the Sermon on the Mount because Matthew 5:43-44 corresponds to Luke 6:27-28.

Jesus teaches us that God provides for believers and unbelievers because He is a provider. The man that receives God's sun and rain did not qualify. God gives sun and rain without fault finding.

God is merciful. He isn't kind to us as payback. He is kind because that is His way. God is not cause and effect. If I believe that God gives me His blessings as payback for my good behavior, at some point I have to accept that it implies He gives me His terror for my wrong.

In His sermon, as recorded in Luke 6, what did Jesus teach His hearers to adopt?

27 But I say unto you which hear, Love your enemies, do good to them which hate you, 28 bless them that curse you, and pray for them which despitefully use you. 29 And unto him that smiteth thee on the one cheek offer also the other; and him that taketh away thy cloak forbid not to take thy coat also. 30 Give to every man that asketh of thee; and of him that taketh away thy goods ask them not again. 31 And as ye would that men should do to you, do ye also to them likewise. 32 For if ye love them which love you, what thank have ye? for sinners also love those that love them. 33 And if ye do good to them which do good to you, what thank have ye? for sinners also do even the same. 34 And if ye lend to them of whom ye hope to receive, what thank have ye? for sinners also lend to sinners, to receive as much again. 35 But love ye your enemies, and do good, and lend, hoping for nothing again; and your reward shall be great, and ye shall be the children of the Highest: for he is kind unto the unthankful and to the evil. 36 Be ye therefore merciful, as your Father also is merciful.

Luke 6:27-36

He taught men to be merciful as God is merciful (v36). The riches of God's mercy causes us to respond in love to our enemies and to show the riches of good works to those who hate us (v27).

He was clear about the characteristics of those under the law:

Hard-hearted men, who do not believe in God's riches, do good to those who do good to them (v33), love those who love them (v32) and lend hoping to receive (v34). The absence of God's riches is why the sinner reciprocates in kind. It is tit for tat.

He then taught that rather than operate like the sinners, we are to operate like our heavenly Father by loving our enemies, doing good, and lending, hoping for nothing again (v35). In contrast to man's ways, God's riches reciprocates not in kind but in opposites. It is not tit for tat with God.

In Luke 6, which is the Sermon on the Mount, Jesus contrasts what life looks like in God's mercy versus what life looks like when the Father's mercy is not correctly interpreted in scriptures. Men resort to living by the law.

Men bring enmity. You bring love to your enemies (v27)

Men bring hatred. You bring good to them which hate you (v27)

Men bring curses. You bring blessing to them which curse you (v29)

Men bring manipulation. You pray for them which despitefully use you (v29)

Again, we see that in contrast to the ways of the hard-hearted unbeliever, the riches of God in His saints reciprocates in opposites and not in kind. Tit-for-tat is not a characteristic of God or the members of His family. This is not will-power.

Thus, as we read through Luke 6, we have to ask ourselves whether what we read is the sinner's method of the law of kinds or the ways of our Father's mercy which is the law of opposites.

Here's Luke 6:38 again:

38 give, and it shall be given unto you; good measure, pressed down, and shaken together, and running over, shall men give into your bosom. For with the same measure that ye mete withal it shall be measured to you again.
Luke 6:37-38

"Give, and it shall be given" is a statement of how the man who rejects God's mercy lives by reciprocating in kind. The men in "shall men give into your bosom" are sinners responding in kind!

Luke 6:38 explains why the earth functions like it does. It is not the way of God or the man who operates in the love of God. Matthew 7:2 corresponds to Luke 6:37-38. It is tit for tat or cause and effect. It is not God in man but man devoid of God.

The man who believes in the riches of God's mercy can see that Jesus teaches His hearers not to operate by Luke 6:38!

Here is an example of what Jesus was teaching:

> *11 The Pharisee stood and prayed thus with himself, God, I thank thee, that I am not as other men are, extortioners, unjust, adulterers, or even as this publican. 12 I fast twice in the week, I give tithes of all that I possess.*
> *Luke 18:11-12*

This Pharisee who wouldn't receive the supply of God's abundant mercy prayed with himself. He was not having fellowship with God. He had no need for God's mercy. He was already righteous (in his own eyes).

This Pharisee gave according to Luke 6:37-38. He gave to bless Himself. He wanted tit-for-tat from God. He needed God to act on the grounds of his own performance. He hoped to obtain righteousness by qualifying himself. Here was one who considered himself a teacher of the scriptures but was peddling the doctrine of men and did not know it! He was proud, blind and lost.

> *13 And the publican, standing afar off, would not lift up so much as his eyes unto heaven, but smote upon his breast, saying, God be merciful to me a sinner. 14 I tell you, this man went down to his house justified rather than the other: for every one that exalteth himself shall be abased; and he that humbleth himself shall be exalted.*
> *Luke 18:13-14*

In the Young's Literal Translation, the publican's confession is "be propitious to me – the sinner".

The Passion Translation says, "God, please, in your mercy and because of the blood sacrifice, forgive me".

That word translated "be merciful" in the KJV is a word that means "supply a sacrifice for my sins." He relied on God's abundant mercy, knowing that God would not relate to him in kind.

He went home justified.

You find God in Luke 6:35-36.

Thankfully, God did not operate Luke 6:38 with us – we did not get what we deserved multiplied back to us. God in man is seen in Christ, who was completely unlike the Luke 6:37-38 man. Jesus was made sin with our sin (2 Corinthians 5:21), died as the just for the unjust (1 Peter 3:18), bore our sins in His own body (1 Peter 2:24), died for us while we were yet sinners (Romans 5:8-10) and is the propitiation for our sins as well as the sins of the whole world (1 John 2:2). Truly, we have seen the mercy of God fully displayed in Christ.

Luke 6:38 is the appeal of selfishness to the man of the senses. It is Luke's contrast of how not to live. The Lord Jesus is showing the light to men who live in Luke 6:38 in order that they may believe that light and move out of the darkness of selfishness.

We give hoping to receive nothing as a result (see Luke 6:33-34). This is because we give as an end in itself and receive because our Father meets our needs. If we give to receive, we operate as the sinner who lends "hoping for something again." The advent of God's nature in men would mean we give to meet the need of others and not as a means of having our own need met.

Luke 6 shows that while people already lived by recompensing evil with evil, good with good and some would even recompense good with evil, Jesus shows that God is not like that. God recompenses both the evil and the good with good. He isn't trying to be nice. That is the way He is. He gives to bless the recipient.

The teaching of Jesus is generosity, which Paul calls the riches of liberality, which is a readiness to distribute because that is the way that God is.

We affirm that the Luke 6:38 "offering time is blessing time" mantra is correct. However, the blessing is two-fold:

It is blessing time for the giver since Jesus said, "it is more blessed to give than to receive" (see Acts 20:35), which means that when you operate in liberality, "ye shall be the children of the Highest: for he is kind unto the unthankful and to the evil" (see Luke 6: 35). Thus, the blessing of the giver is the freedom to express the riches of the liberality, which is God's riches in His saints. We are free of covetousness.

It is also blessing time for the receiver of the riches of the liberality of the giver in that a need is met.

It is not blessing time in that the one doing the giving turns the act of giving into a casino experience where the offering bowl is an investment mechanism, a hedge fund for managing your money and increasing your portfolio. When we reason that the blessing in "blessing time" is for the one doing the giving, we awaken the love of money, which veils liberality in the saint.

Peter rebuked this casino approach:

18 And when Simon saw that through laying on of the apostles' hands the Holy Ghost was given, he offered them money, 19 saying, Give me also this power, that on whomsoever I lay hands, he may receive the Holy Ghost. 20 But Peter said unto him, Thy money perish with thee, because thou hast thought that the gift of God may be purchased with money. 21 Thou hast neither part nor lot in this matter: for thy heart is not right in the sight of God. 22 Repent therefore of this thy wickedness, and pray God, if perhaps the thought of thine heart may be forgiven thee. 23 For I perceive that thou art in the gall of bitterness, and in the bond of iniquity.

Acts 8:18-23

Some defend the idea of giving hoping to get back as a way of exercising faith in God's provisions. What some might call faith, Peter rightly identified as a heart not right with God!

Could Simon be "sowing" into Peter's ministry to tap into that power at work in Peter? Could it be that Peter would honour Simon's "faith" since Simon wanted to minister to people so they too might receive the spirit through Simon's ministry? Peter's response settled this forever. He said, "Thy money perish with thee, because thou hast thought that the gift of God may be purchased with money." Peter rebuked Simon's "giving", which hoped to receive something (power) based on giving. Simon wanted to use his giving to receive what God gave freely. That is covetousness. That mentality reflects a heart that is not right with God.

Peter couldn't see Simon's "faith" nor would he honor it.

The saint doesn't live in Luke 6:38 for it describes a heart that is not right with God.

We give. We get. We do not give to get.

13

That shall he also reap

7. Be not deceived; God is not mocked: for whatsoever a man soweth, that shall he also reap.
Galatians 6:7

This text does not prove that God reciprocates in kind rather than in opposites. But this doesn't describe God. God is not active but inactive. It is the activity of man.

Counted worthy of double honour

6. Let him that is taught in the word communicate unto him that teacheth in all good things.
Galatians 6:6

The saint that has been blessed spiritually by the riches of God's word through a minister should, "communicate unto him that teacheth in all good things". The term "all good things" refers to material things.

The scripture teaches that the labourer is worthy of his reward or wages.

17. Let the elders that rule well be counted worthy of double honour, especially

they who labour in the word and doctrine. 18. For the scripture saith, Thou shalt not muzzle the ox that treadeth out the corn. And, The labourer is worthy of his reward.
1 Timothy 5:17-18

We give to ministers in honour of God because the scripture says that the labourer is worthy of his reward or wages. New Testament giving is based on honour. When we give to the minister, we are honouring God by honouring the minister who has laboured in God's word. The writer of Hebrews describes submission as the riches that we give to those who labour over us in the word (see Hebrews 13:17). Observe that Paul does not promise the saint monetary reward for giving to the minister. Promising more money for expressing the riches of generosity is not a New Testament slant. Such promises use fair speeches to make merchandise of the saints. We give to ministers to enrich them and not as a means for the giver to get more money. Saints give based on honour and not on seeing giving as an avenue to yet more material riches for the saint.

It was to these saints who Paul had told to count ministers who labour in the word worthy of double honour that he encouraged to practice the riches of good works. They had become rich without being liberal givers (see 1 Timothy 6:17-18) and their failure to give had not caused their wealth to vaporise. They already knew that they do not get rich by giving to others. The reality is that just as there are rich people that give to others, there are many more rich people that do not. Money will flow towards the saint on account of knowing how the systems of the earth operates independent of the saint's giving.

Let us also walk in the Spirit

Paul's "let him communicate unto him that teacheth in all good things" is how to practice "If we live in the Spirit, let us also walk in the Spirit" (see Galatians 5:25). This "if" is the same as "since", given that "living in the spirit" is not in doubt. This is an "if" of reality." The saint lives in the spirit. The word translated "walk" means to keep in step with another that sets the pace. We keep in line with God's love for us. To walk in the spirit is to walk in step with love's lead. Love here is agape, which is a life totally committed to another. It correctly describes God's capacity to share – that which was received by each saint in the New Birth.

22. But the fruit of the Spirit is love, joy, peace, longsuffering, gentleness, goodness, faith, 23. Meekness, temperance: against such there is no law.
Galatians 5:22 - 23

Paul describes the riches of God's spirit in each saint and then proceeds to explain what keeping in step with love's lead looks like in different scenarios.

His first example was to show that love would show itself as the riches of meekness, which restores the brother who is overtaken in a fault (see Galatians 6:1). The teachers of "another gospel", who teach the doctrine of the Pharisees, would demand "just recompense for every transgression." They'll teach tit-for-tat, which is not the law of love but the law of sin and death. The tragedy of the teaching of covetousness is that rather than train the saint in the riches of mercy, it uses saints to administer condemnation to other saints. The doctrine of Christ is to "restore such a one." Paul is contrasting how love would show itself as the riches of meekness instead of the punishment for sins.

The love that shows up as the riches of meekness would also show itself as the riches of goodness to ministers who have taught the saints the riches of God's grace. This is the riches of liberality that gives. Paul is giving one continuous teaching about the love-walk from the previous chapter. "Walking in the spirit" means supplying the riches of this world to those who have taught the gospel to us. The saint gives the riches of this world because that is what the fruit of the spirit will express itself as in that scenario.

Two categories of teachers

Paul's instructions to the Galatian saints about expressing the riches of liberality to ministers who labour in the word involves discernment, since he has contrasted the effect of two types of teachers in his letter to the Galatians.

2. This only would I learn of you, Received ye the Spirit by the works of the law, or by the hearing of faith? 3. Are ye so foolish? having begun in the Spirit, are ye now made perfect by the flesh?
Galatians 3:2 - 3

The saints had received the spirit by the hearing of faith and not by the works of the law. The hearing of faith is the correct explanation of those utterances of the prophets that were to produce faith in their hearers. This he refers to as "having begun in the Spirit", which is receiving the spirit as the riches of salvation.

The "works of the law" refers to the hardened heart attempting to practice ordinances rather than believe the message of faith. This is the end result of the doctrine of the Pharisees, who peddle myths, old wives' fables and the commandments of men. This explanation promotes being "made perfect by the flesh" and it is this doctrine ministered by those ministers he had earlier referred to as troublemakers (see Galatians 5:10). These are the ministers "whose mouths must be stopped" (see Titus 1:11).

It is most interesting that Paul pointedly avoids naming Moses anywhere in the book of Galatians. He treats Moses as a minister of the gospel.

Therefore, when we read "let him that is taught in the word communicate unto him that teacheth in all good things", we are to discern which ministers Paul would have the saints recognise as "him that teacheth." Is he telling the saints to support those troublemaking ministers (Galatians 5:10) that he had referred to as "many unruly and vain talkers … specially they of the circumcision who teach things which they ought not, for filthy lucre's sake"? (see Titus 1: 10-11). The Galatian saints are to discern which ministries they are to submit themselves to.

A little leaven

The particular liberty that Paul went to war about in Galatians was the teaching of circumcision. The ordinance of circumcision itself points to the heart that believes. In unbelief, the hardened heart holds on to the ordinance while rejecting faith in the gospel. He said that to concede ground to those teaching circumcision was to allow bondage in the church (see Galatians 2:4,12; 5:2). Today, many wouldn't consider that such an "unimportant" issue as circumcision demanded a book, much less an apostolic epistle.

Why this all-guns-blazing stance from Paul?

9. A little leaven leaveneth the whole lump.
Galatians 5: 9

Paul admitted that he had made a big deal out of "a little leaven."

Jesus had referred to the doctrine of the Pharisees and of the Sadducees as leaven (Matthew 16: 11 – 12), for they explained scriptures in ways that imposed a burden on their hearers when they should have repented by teaching the way Jesus taught. The scriptures do not produce bondage, it is the "Sadducees and Pharisees" explanation that does. The Sadducees and Pharisees interpreted the scriptures in a way that took away the liberty hard-fought and won in Christ's sacrifice.

Paul's point was that if we allow the "little" matter of circumcision remain unchallenged, it won't be long before the doctrine of Christ would be completely wiped out of people's consciousness and legalism follows with the more dangerous covetousness in tow.

He that soweth

8. For he that soweth to his flesh shall of the flesh reap corruption; but he that soweth to the Spirit shall of the Spirit reap life everlasting.
Galatians 6: 8

Paul had said "they that are Christ's have crucified the flesh with the affections and lusts" (see Galatians 5: 24). The flesh has been crucified in the sacrifice of Christ - The flesh is not the body.

He that "soweth to his flesh" would be he that does not walk in the spirit, which refers to the saint who doesn't follow love's lead. In the light of the overall message of Galatians, sowing to the flesh means departing from our identity in Christ. The one who sows to the flesh is not walking like a saint who has received the riches of God's goodness in salvation. In context, this would be failure to minister the riches of goodness to one's teacher.

What happens when one does not minister the riches of goodness to one's teacher (one who sows to the flesh)?

Paul says such a saint would reap corruption.

In his letters, Paul used corruption in relation to false doctrine and to describe the mortal body. This means that there is no fixed meaning that can be attached to the word "corruption" to fit all instances. We decipher its meaning from context.

Paul used corruption to refer to the mortal body, which "is sown in corruption ... raised in incorruption". He was explaining the resurrection of the dead (see 1 Corinthians 15:42). He taught the guarantee of a glorified body to all saints when he said, "this corruptible must put on incorruption, and this mortal must put on immortality (see 1 Corinthians 15:53, Romans 8:21). Since the glorified body is the blessed hope guaranteed to all saints, the saint reaping corruption cannot be failure to obtain an incorruptible body.

The word translated as corruption has also been translated "perish" in "which all are to perish with the using; after the commandments and doctrines of men?" (see Colossians 2:22). Thus, Paul also used corruption in relation to those doctrines that are classified as the commandment of men.

The corruption due to teaching the commandment of men is addressed in Colossians 2:18 (this is a text that requires attention).

18 Let no one defraud you of your prize [your freedom in Christ and your salvation] by insisting on mock humility and the worship of angels, going into detail about visions [he claims] he has seen [to justify his authority], puffed up [in conceit] by his unspiritual mind,
Colossians 2:18 (AMP)

The Amplified version sees the prize as already guaranteed. It is salvation and liberty in Christ. Seeing that salvation is guaranteed, the man who believes the gospel would laugh at the criticisms of the minister that condemns those not practicing their false ideas. Don't take such criticisms seriously. The prize is certain.

The margin of the Holman Christian Standard Bible gives an alternate reading "let no one cheat us out of your prize". The idea is that of a fellow competitor hindering you to the extent that you start believing the criticisms passed by those who peddle wrong doctrine. This affects you and causes you to abandon the impulses of the new nature and the truth of God's word. You get cheated out of your prize. You forfeit your prize. This would be the loss of reward.

Paul teaches a lot about the concept of rewards:

Paul said, "But I keep under my body, and bring it into subjection: lest that by any means, when I have preached to others, I myself should be a castaway" (see 1 Corinthians 9: 27). In the NIV, it reads "No, I strike a blow to my body and make it my slave so that after I have preached to others, I myself will not be disqualified for the prize". Paul meant that he faced the danger of the loss of rewards. He instructs the saint to run so as to win that prize. While athletes obtain the reward of a corruptible crown, the saint receives an incorruptible (see 1 Corinthians 9:25).

He also covers this idea in 1 Corinthians 3. He said, "if any man's work shall be burned, he shall suffer loss: but he himself shall be saved; yet so as by fire" (see 1 Corinthians 3:15). The saint is the work of Christ. Christ's work will not be judged. Therefore, the saint does not lose salvation. It is the work of the saint that is being judged. The burning of those works refers to the saint forfeiting eternal rewards. It is suffering the loss of an incorruptible reward that is "corruption." The man is not being punished for his bad works. Paul's "shall of the flesh reap corruption" describes the saint suffering the loss of an eternal or incorruptible reward.

Since Paul presented "shall of the flesh reap corruption" as the opposite of "shall of the Spirit reap life everlasting," and we have established that "reap corruption" means suffer the loss of eternal rewards, "reap life everlasting" means receive eternal rewards. This happens when all saints appear before the judgment seat of Christ to receive eternal rewards (see 2 Corinthians 5:10).

The Lord had instructed, "lay not up for yourselves treasures upon earth" (see Matthew 6:19). Instead, you "lay up for yourselves treasures in heaven" (see Matthew 6:20). Therefore, to "reap life everlasting" could not be about laying up earthly treasures as reward. The rewards for walking in the spirit cannot be perishable or uncertain riches like money. They are eternal rewards. To make the rewards for walking in the new nature money, would be to say that the reward for walking in the spirit is corruptible or perishable riches!

Paul's "he that soweth to the Spirit shall of the Spirit reap life everlasting" means the saint would reap eternal rewards for walking in step with love's leading. In context, this walk has been expressed as the riches of liberality towards ministers in honour of their labour in the word.

When do we reap? We reap in due season.

Due season is when we appear before the judgment seat of Christ (see 2 Corinthians 5:20). We will reap in that we go onto our rewards for not fainting in the love walk.

He has given us His spirit. We do not faint in ministering the riches of liberality and when our works are judged before the judgment seat, we receive eternal rewards.

Prior to the judgment seat of Christ

Are there ongoing effects before we stand before the judgment seat of Christ?

Paul's warning to the saints was, "you are so soon removed from him that called you into the grace of Christ unto another gospel: Which is not another; but there be some that trouble you, and would pervert the gospel of Christ" (see Galatians 1:6-7).

The word translated "trouble you" means bring you agitations, disturb your inner peace, take away your inner calm, confuse you, make you restless and perplex your mind. Saints should continually use the doctrine of Christ by which they have received the New Birth to judge everything else that anyone preaches to them. We must not accept the cunning logic of materialism and legalism.

This is like Acts 15:

24. Forasmuch as we have heard, that certain which went out from us have troubled you with words, subverting your souls, saying, Ye must be circumcised, and keep the law: to whom we gave no such commandment:
Acts 15: 24

Notice that "certain which went out from us" are saints who accepted the doctrine of Christ for salvation but teach the doctrine of the Pharisees for all else. Their explanations of scriptures trouble the saints by confusing them. Their message was anti-Christ for it made the saints restless by disturbing that inner peace which they had received by believing the gospel. The "trouble" given through preaching was received in the hearing of the saints. Saints develop persuasions based on what they have heard over time, even if that persuasion hinders their spiritual growth. Paul called this foolishness (see Galatians 3:2). The inability or unwillingness to use what has already been taught to judge all else that is being taught is foolishness.

They had heard Paul preach Christ's mode of explanation as gospel and almost as soon as they heard and believed it, they did not continue in it by pressing into understanding it and reasoning from that way of explaining scriptures. They succumbed to the explanation called cunningly devised fables, which distracted and diverted into "another gospel." This "another gospel" is unbelief that rejects Christ as the interpreter and interpretation of scriptures.

To these saints that he said were foolish and bewitched (see Galatians 3:1) and removed to "another gospel", Paul's solution was to remind them of God's grace in Christ (see Galatians 1:3). He is referring to the initial presentation of the doctrine of Christ by which they had received the riches of salvation.

He reminded them of how he had presented the gospel to them by saying, "before whose eyes Jesus Christ hath been evidently set forth" (see Galatians 3: 1).

The Greek word translated "hath been evidently set forth" is translated as "things written aforetime" in Romans 15:4. Also translated "as I wrote before" in Ephesians 3:3. Scholars say it means "to write before the eyes of all who can read". It refers to the faith-giving utterances of the prophets written previously. Paul's point is that the message found in Christ's mode of explaining those faith-giving scriptures is to interpret the things written to reveal peace and rest as God's gift in Christ. They should have seen that God was obligated to do what they were trying to do. They were to believe.

If the saints accept another interpretation asides that explanation found in the doctrine of Christ they would have been removed from the gospel of Christ.

"You are so soon removed" shows that there is a consequence that shows up in our lives on account of the doctrine we expose ourselves to. The human heart produces in line with whatever doctrine it has been exposed to – even if it is "another gospel." The import is that, the effect of supporting the preaching of "another gospel" is not neutral on the heart. The saint that supports ministers who contradict the "hearing of faith" sets himself up to living by will-power and not the activity of the spirit within.

What if these ministers are preaching a revelation received through supernatural means?

Hear Paul:

8. But though we, or an angel from heaven, preach any other gospel unto you than that which we have preached unto you, let him be accursed. 9. As we said before, so say I now again, If any man preach any other gospel unto you than that ye have received, let him be accursed.
Galatians 1: 8 - 9

"Angel from heaven" refers to spectacular origins of revelation. We are to judge all things by "that ye have received." That is apostolic teaching. It is the standard by which Paul said even his own ministry was to be judged.

We judge supernatural and spectacular operations in the light of that interpretation which was preached to us at the beginning. We don't use angels' words to understand the Gospel. We use the explanation found in Christ's doctrine to understand, judge and discern angelic encounters.

What should we do if the message is contrary to the truth of salvation in Christ?

Paul said to do something about the minister. He said "let him be accursed." That expression doesn't mean that we place a curse on the minister – that would be demonic! He means that the minister will receive the consequences of his ministerial actions, which he explains in other scriptures when dealing with similar issues.

17. Now I beseech you, brethren, mark them which cause divisions and offences contrary to the doctrine which ye have learned; and avoid them.
Romans 16: 17

"Let them be accursed" means to mark those which cause "divisions and offences contrary to the doctrine" which we have learned. In those scenarios "accursed" means we should mark them and avoid them (see Titus 3:10). This means "set his teachings aside." Have nothing to do with such teachings. Those subtle poisons that appear to teach the sacrifice of Christ, the new creation, and additional things that amount to the law! Treat it as accursed – don't touch it.

Paul's warning implies that our ministry to the saints after they have received the riches of salvation is to establish the saint in that gospel which had been preached to them at the beginning. The preacher that preaches anything that deviates from the thing preached to the saints at the beginning is walking disorderly. Our scriptural response in love is to set aside those things that he is saying.

What did Paul preach?

In his own words, he said "Remember that Jesus Christ of the seed of David was raised from the dead according to my gospel: Wherein I suffer trouble, as an evil doer, even unto bonds; but the word of God is not bound" (see 2 Timothy 2: 8 - 9)

All that Paul taught was an explanation of that resurrection and his explanations brought him much trouble from people who labelled him an evil doer.

What evil did he do that made them label him an "evil doer"?

Paul's evil deed, was the evil of establishing the saints in peace and assuring their hearts by explaining the resurrection of Christ as the fulfilment of the utterance of the prophets.

Paul's "having begun in the Spirit, are ye now made perfect by the flesh?" (see Galatians 3: 3) is because the Galatians had begun to grow spiritually by paying heed exclusively to the doctrine of Christ. However, by also listening to that perversion of the gospel called the doctrine of the Pharisees, which is another gospel, it was impossible for them to grow spiritually. Paul implies that the purpose of the gospel is not just right conduct by any means. It is important to establish whether the origin of their acts was a product of spiritual growth or will worship arising from compliance with the law. It is not merely acting right, it should be the riches of good works by walking in the spirit, which acknowledges God's work in men.

There is a false "love walk" that gives to support the doctrine of the Pharisees. This only ministers more mental and psychological agitation to the saints. It opens those mouths that should be shut and is therefore a violation of the law of love.

16. Hereby perceive we the love of God, because he laid down his life for us: and we ought to lay down our lives for the brethren. 17. But whoso hath this world's good, and seeth his brother have need, and shutteth up his bowels of compassion from him, how dwelleth the love of God in him?
1 John 3: 16 - 17

John said, "we ought to lay down our lives for the brethren". He means that the same sacrificial love seen in Christ compels us to care for other saints. Thus, if we see our brother, who teaches the Law, have need, we do not shut up the bowels of compassion from him. We come to his aid if he is in difficulty, for he is a saint. He is our brother.

However, we do not support the ministry of the "works of the law," which speaks contrary to Christ by adding the law to the grace of our Lord Jesus. If we do so, we would be enabling the leaven that leavens the whole lump.

Be not deceived

6. Let him that is taught in the word communicate unto him that teacheth in all good things. 7. Be not deceived; God is not mocked: for whatsoever a man soweth, that shall he also reap. 8. For he that soweth to his flesh shall of the flesh reap corruption; but he that soweth to the Spirit shall of the Spirit reap life everlasting. 9. And let us not be weary in well doing: for in due season we shall reap, if we faint not.
Galatians 6: 6 - 9

The love of God which had been showcased as the riches of meekness in restoring the brother caught in a fault, is also expressed as the riches of goodness to ministers who have taught the saints the riches of God's grace. The riches of liberality honours ministers by giving to them. This is our sane contribution to the increase of persuasion amongst men concerning the power of God's love.

God's spirit received in the New Birth is the ability to share the riches of generosity. Those taught the doctrine of Christ receive persuasion to excel in that generosity. If the same saint listens to the doctrine of the Pharisees, persuasion concerning covetousness increases.

If in expressing generosity towards your teacher, you are sponsoring that which teaches or preaches the doing of the Law instead of (or in addition to) walking in the spirit, such doctrine will affect your heart-slant and increase your departure from the love walk. The consequence is that the works of the flesh (see Galatians 5) will become dominant through the misplaced generosity of the saint. In the scenario where the saint mixes the doctrine of grace with the law, that "little leaven" will leaven the whole lump and the heart of the saint never becomes established in the truth of the gospel. Mixing the law with grace never results in the proper understanding of grace and worse still, it prevents growth in grace and leads to regression. Any attempt at such a mixture would result in a return to legalism powered by materialism and confidence in the hearts about liberty in Christ evaporates – it leavens the whole lump!

What is this corruption in the present?

This troubling of the mind that removes persuasion about God's love or the setting aside of our hard-won liberty in Christ is the corruption that happens in the present before the other corruption that happens when we appear before the judgment seat of Christ.

What should have been reaped?

Love should have shown up as the riches of liberality, riches of goodness and patience. Instead, the saint will be removed from the liberty that is in Christ and would be tangled with the yoke of bondage again. Soon, the saint stops giving to honour the teacher and starts giving to get more money in a performance-based works system. This means that the spiritual growth that should have proceeded from feeding on the diet of the truth of the grace of Christ will not happen.

In the present, this corruption is the loss of spiritual growth.

The one reaping of loss of spiritual growth is the saint who has been supporting ministries which preach the law in addition to grace. In receiving that diet, the saint receives agitation into the mind and loses persuasion about the love of God in Christ. The saint wants to earn what has been freely given or worse still use giving to get ahead financially (which is impossible). Such a saint who sows to the flesh is ignoring the new nature. Whatever that saint gives is not the riches of liberality for it isn't born out of the love walk.

Such a saint would not walk in the new nature.

Since spiritual growth comes from yielding to the new nature, such a saint will not grow spiritually. Saints who do not listen to the riches of God's grace will have their heart feasting on the bondage of the Law which robs them of enjoying the true liberty hard won in Christ. They have sown to the flesh by giving heed to the Law. They reap corruption in that all that they would have been taught would be nothing that is fit to produce spiritual growth. The New Birth is with spiritual growth in mind. To receive the New Birth and not pursue spiritual growth is corruption.

On the other hand, those very saints could support ministries that would teach them the supply of the spirit through Christ's sacrifice and that will cause them to live out the supply of God through them to bless others. This would be seen in the emergence of the fruit of the spirit – the riches of God in His saints. The saint who has been supporting ministries which preach the grace of Christ, receives that sound diet and continues in it, will reap spiritual growth, which is the life everlasting of the spirit.

Saints who assume that they are growing but who do not actively support those ministries that teach them the riches of the spirit supplied through Christ's sacrifice are deceived (see Galatians 6:6-7). After receiving the rich ministry of God's word, a saint would respond by giving to that minister. Giving to those ministers who teach you the word opens up your heart to receive what has been taught. The honour flowing from you to them has that influence on your heart as the recipient of the riches of God's word.

The correct response to receiving the riches of God's word is not to tell the minister, "Man of God that was solid word." Saints who do that think they prioritise the word but they don't.

If a poor minister teaches the riches of God's grace to you, you give to that minister because of honour for the work done in labouring over you in the word. If a rich minister teaches the same riches to you, you still respond with the riches of liberality. You are giving independent of the minister's financial status.

So, prior to the judgement seat of Christ:

"Be not deceived; God is not mocked" means that a saint can reap corruption (agitation, confusion and perplexity of the mind that hinders the emergence of spiritual growth) or reap everlasting life (receive spiritual growth by receiving and continuing in the diet of the grace of Christ).

The well doing in "let us not be weary in well doing" refers to walking in the spirit by supporting ministries that advance the ministration of the spirit. Be a minister of the spirit. Be one who actively gives towards those type of ministries. It establishes the saints in peace and keeps your heart free of greed.

At the judgement seat of Christ, "be not deceived; God is not mocked" is receiving eternal rewards or suffering the loss of it.

14

Contentment is great gain

Perhaps, the most overlooked effect of eternal life in man is contentment.

10. But I rejoiced in the Lord greatly, that now at the last your care of me hath flourished again; wherein ye were also careful, but ye lacked opportunity. 11. Not that I speak in respect of want: for I have learned, in whatsoever state I am, therewith to be content.
Philippians 4: 10 - 11

These are the words of a man who had "learned in whatsoever state I am, therewith to be content." Contentment is a joyful disposition in the victory of Christ. Contentment is the Christian's calm confidence in God's riches irrespective of outcomes or circumstances.

He was rejoicing greatly that the doctrine of Christ was bearing fruit in the saints in that they had shared material riches with those who had blessed them with the riches of God's word without any motivation induced by covetousness.

17. Not because I desire a gift: but I desire fruit that may abound to your account.
Philippians 4: 17

The word translated "account" is the Greek logos, which refers to the gospel message that Paul had taught them. The message had watered the riches of generosity that was God's gift to the saint in the New Birth. Paul's desire was to see the gospel reproduce in the saints at Philippi the same riches of liberality seen in the sacrifice of Christ. It was the doctrine bearing fruit rather than the saints responding to manipulation, covetousness or coercion. The fruit that may abound to their account is the message producing in the saints. The same generosity seen in Christ, given through the New Birth, and taught through the gospel is now seen in these saints. Whereas, saints can be schooled to give in response to shame and guilt, and it would appear that such saints were givers. The giving that arises from being merchandised with fair speeches would stop the true fruit of the gospel coming forth. Giving should be an expression of the generosity of God flowing out through the saint.

As a minister of the gospel, Paul was keen for his hearers to understand his motive. He steered clear of covetousness in his methods because people respond to covetousness in the minister. Paul jealously guarded against this.

15. Now ye Philippians know also, that in the beginning of the gospel, when I departed from Macedonia, no church communicated with me as concerning giving and receiving, but ye only.
Philippians 4:15

This giving and receiving is not by the same people.

The Philippians did the giving. Paul did the receiving.

The people wanted to give to Paul but the opportunity was lacking. They lived in a day and age where the logistics of getting supplies to those in need often involved exposing people to physical danger.

While they lacked opportunity, Paul had contentment.

Paul did not write the other churches to blast them for not giving to him like the Philippians! He rejoiced with the Philippians who gave to him personally, while using the liberality of the Macedonians to remind the other saints that the same power was in them. Contentment prevented him from artificially increasing the saints' giving by preaching the doctrine of the Pharisees to them.

12. I know both how to be abased, and I know how to abound: every where and in all things I am instructed both to be full and to be hungry, both to abound and to suffer need. 13. I can do all things through Christ which strengtheneth me.
Philippians 4:12 - 13

"All things" refers to the conditions of abundance or lack that Paul had stated in verse 12.

"I can do" refers to the ability to reign over covetousness. It describes the saint whose joy remained steady independent of support from others. Paul is saying, "I remain in joy whether I suffer need or you give to meet my need." Paul wanted the Philippians to know that he knew how to handle their giving to him as well as when their gifts were absent.

"Christ which strengtheneth me" refers to contentment at work in Paul. Contentment is the ability to stay at rest on the inside independent of supply or lack on the outside. This is freedom to stay free of anxiety.

Here is what Paul told Timothy:

5. Perverse disputings of men of corrupt minds, and destitute of the truth, supposing that gain is godliness: from such withdraw thyself. 6. But godliness with contentment is great gain.
1 Timothy 6:5 – 6

The "gain" in "gain is godliness" refers to material wealth. It is not revelation knowledge to teach that gain is godliness. That teaching reveals a corrupt mind which is destitute of the truth of God's Word. Teaching that having money or being poor is a measure of spirituality is departure from apostolic teaching. Material wealth is independent of spirituality and not because of it. The scriptures show that God confers spirituality through the gospel. Timothy is to withdraw himself from ministers who place a spiritual value on the acquisition or loss of wealth. As a saint, you cannot be responsible for what others teach but you are responsible for the doctrine that you submit yourself to. If Timothy does not withdraw himself from such teaching they have a way of making sense after a while thus corrupting his mind from the simplicity which is in Christ.

Since we have the rich and the poor among both the saints and sinners, it doesn't make sense to attach spirituality to financial gain. There's no use denying that many sinners have loads of money. Whether one has money or not depends on many other factors asides godliness.

Gain is not godliness. Financial gain is economic and not spiritual. It is the way of man.

Paul teaches that godliness with contentment is great gain. "Great gain" means that the saint is to see contentment as true riches. True riches are independent of material wealth. Rather than revere saints on account of their material wealth, we celebrate those saints who remain the same independent of the presence or the absence of money. We make a big deal of the true riches of contentment.

It is in our knowledge of God in Christ (godliness) that we find contentment. Contentment means that we recognize that there is no further clarification of God's ways other than His way as seen in the incarnation, the work of Christ and His doctrine. The heart is fully nourished in contentment as it sees Christ as the revelation of God. Contentment is the barometer of the riches of God's inheritance within the saint. It is to be cultivated and given a large place in our thinking instead of surrendering our minds to teachings which promote covetousness (the idea of interpreting financial power as reward for spirituality).

The minister of the gospel does not major on financial gain or loss. Contentment would mean that I find peace in obeying God whether my finances improve as a result of such obedience or not. The reward of obedience is sensitivity to God. Obedience is an end in itself.

7. For we brought nothing into this world, and it is certain we can carry nothing out.
1 Timothy 6: 7

Although, the earth is the Lord's and its fulness, we do not trust material riches. It is weird that many only learn the futility of material riches at death. However, we don't need to die to learn these lessons that way. The gospel teaches us not to trust in uncertain riches. Since godliness with contentment is true riches, the godly man who has cultivated contentment carries contentment beyond this life.

Here's Paul's forgotten warning to Timothy:

9. But they that will be rich fall into temptation and a snare, and into many foolish and hurtful lusts, which drown men in destruction and perdition 10. For the love of money is the root of all evil: which while some coveted after, they have erred from the faith, and pierced themselves through with many sorrows
1 Timothy 6: 9-10

Paul's "they that will be rich fall into temptation and a snare" does not mean that he is set against saints getting ahead in life or improving their lot in life – that wouldn't make sense. The man who goes to the market place does so with the intention of making money. That is intelligent. "They that will be rich" is another term for covetousness, "the love of money", or "hurtful lusts". "They that will be rich" refers to giving oneself over to covetousness. In context, Paul's expression "love of money" refers to the evil of ministering the gospel for material gain. Such love would successfully corrupt the minister's message. The love of money births those hurtful desires that facilitate saints falling into greed. We do not preach the gospel as a means to get money.

James throws some light on the true riches:

9. Let the brother of low degree rejoice in that he is exalted: 10. But the rich, in that he is made low: because as the flower of the grass he shall pass away.
James 1: 9-10

James speaks of two brothers one "of low degree" and the other "the rich." Both are brothers in Christ. The descriptions "low degree" and "rich" have no bearing on their salvation. The brother of "low degree" is the naked and destitute brother, in "if a brother or sister be naked, and destitute of daily food" (see James 2: 15). Thus, low degree is destitute or lacking in material wealth. This is the financially poor saint.

James did not say that the brother of low degree is poor because he has failed to receive financial wealth from the sacrifice of Christ. A bona fide saint in Christ can be "naked, and destitute of daily food". The idea of money as inheritance in Christ is foreign to the gospel, therefore it does not come up in James' letter at all. Jesus did not bear our financial poverty on the cross. The implication is that the sacrifice of Christ did not confer "low degree" or "rich" on anyone.

The brother who is financially poor is instructed to "rejoice in that he is exalted". This exaltation did not stop him from being "naked, and destitute of daily food". His rejoicing is not the celebration of financial poverty. Instead, he rejoices in that he is exalted. This exaltation is a reference to true wealth in Christ. James did not tell the "brother of low degree" to rejoice his destitution or poverty away. This brother rejoices in the exaltation that is founded on true riches in Christ because that is the saint's confidence. This is contentment.

In the Epistles, we see that the term "rich" when applied to God has a meaning other than financial. The Epistles measure God's riches as His being "rich unto all", which means that God has enough resources to supply His salvation to all that call upon Him (see Romans 10: 12 – 13). His riches are described as His mercy, which is His love that quickened us together with Christ (see Ephesians 2:4), as the forgiveness of sins through His blood (see Ephesians 1:7), as His kindness towards us (see Ephesians 2: 7), as His glory which is permanent cleansing from sin as His inheritance in the saints (see Ephesians 1: 18), as His goodness which is seen in His forbearance and longsuffering which changes our mind (see Romans 2: 4), as suffering reproach for Christ and ministering to others (see Hebrews 11:24-26).

James instructs the rich saint to see material wealth as being made low. This "made low" is better translated as made lower. Material wealth is lower than the exaltation that is founded on true riches in Christ, which is a form of wealth common to both the poor brother and the rich brother. James isn't against the rich brother, he is simply making the big point that material riches are not the spiritual blessings in Christ.

In James 1: 10, what passes away is the material riches of the rich. "In his ways" refers to the man's possessions. The apostles speak as though material riches are in man's hands while spiritual riches are in God's hands. It is certain that material riches will not be eternal. They are uncertain. They pass away. It is the riches of salvation as God's eternal inheritance that delivers man from emptiness. It is God's riches that makes man a recipient of things eternal, otherwise all else is nothing.

1. For the sun is no sooner risen with a burning heat, but it withereth the grass, and the flower thereof falleth, and the grace of the fashion of it perisheth: so also shall the rich man fade away in his ways.
James 1: 11

James' "so also shall the rich man fade away in his ways" refers to the non-permanent nature of material wealth. It fades away. Material wealth is not of an enduring quality like the riches of God's mercy, which is Christ supplied as wealth in every saint.

Combining James insight with Paul's admonition to Timothy, we see that covetousness produces hurtful lusts that bewitches the saint into seeing material wealth in Christ's sacrifice. It makes many saints ignore the true riches of contentment. The saint should enjoy material wealth while building his or her confidence on the supply of the true wealth in Christ, which is the perfect gift from above. The true riches "cometh down from the Father of lights" (see James 1: 17). Contentment fixes our gaze on the eternal riches of salvation.

15

Giving to a Man of God

17. Let the elders that rule well be counted worthy of double honour, especially they who labour in the word and doctrine. 18. For the scripture saith, Thou shalt not muzzle the ox that treadeth out the corn. And, The labourer is worthy of his reward.

1 Timothy 5: 17-18

Saints who are not persuaded about God's nature tend to give out of fear that God would punish them with financial poverty if they did not give. When some of these saints find out that God isn't that way, they stop giving. Their only motivation had been fear.

Saints give as the practice of honour. We can tell that we prioritize the message by giving to support the messenger. It is dishonour not to give to the minister who has laboured in God's word. In practice, there is very little difference, if any at all, between those who oppose the message of a preacher and those who don't give to the preacher.

Paul had told the Macedonian (Philippian) saints, "no church communicated with me as concerning giving and receiving, but ye only" (see Philippians 4: 15). What did he say to the saints at Philippi who had given to Paul's ministry in a way no other assembly matched?

19. But my God shall supply all your need according to his riches in glory by Christ Jesus.

Philippians 4: 19

He said that God supplies all their need according to His riches by Christ Jesus. Although some think that he said so, Paul did not say, "My God shall meet your need because you have given to me." If he had said that, it would mean that God keeps a vigil on our giving as a trigger for Him to provide for us.

Paul's point was that God meets our need. He does this His way. His way is to supply by Christ. All that God does was done in, and by Christ's sacrifice. Paul is not saying that God would only meet the need of the Philippians while He leaves the other churches to suffer. That's not the way of God.

9. Not because we have not power, but to make ourselves an ensample unto you to follow us.
2 Thessalonians 3: 9

The love of God makes each saint see that they continually give to the man who labours over them in the word. However, the man who labours in the word should not see it as mandatory to receive the gifts of the saints. While it is true that the saints should continually improve in ministering material riches to those who labour over them in the word, it is up to the minister to receive it or not to. A minister should not see it as mandatory to receive his needs met through saints responding back in carnal things. Ministers can choose to follow Paul's example by receiving their needs met through other means.

Paul let these saints know that it was expected that they give to support him. However, he deliberately subordinated that right and made it secondary to ensuring that they saw a clear example of honest living in him. He saw that the best way to be an example of industry and hard work to the saints at Thessalonica was by working a secular job and not receiving gifts from them.

The fact that Paul told the Corinthians, "Have we not power to lead about a sister, a wife, as well as other apostles, and as the brethren of the Lord, and Cephas? Or I only and Barnabas, have not we power to forbear working?" (see 1 Corinthians 9: 5 - 6), means that Paul knew that the Corinthians assumed that they were to support only the apostles of the Lamb and that since Paul wasn't an apostle of the Lamb, there was no need to support him.

He taught them the truth:

11. If we have sown unto you spiritual things, is it a great thing if we shall reap your carnal things?
1 Corinthians 9: 11

Ordinarily, those who preach the gospel should live off it. There is nothing in all of God's word against that.

Some would have anticipated that Paul would then follow up that logic with "I am changing my tactic. From now onwards start giving to me for it is my right." However, Paul wasn't going to coerce or manipulate them into increasing their giving. Instead, Paul wanted it to be clear that his motivation for ministering the riches of Christ was not covetousness – a minister should watch his motive for teaching giving! Therefore, although "the Lord ordained that they which preach the gospel should live of the gospel", Paul chose not to exercise the Lord's provision that ministers are to be supported with the material provisions of those who have received rich ministry from them. The Lord had ordained it but had not demanded it of the minister. It is not mandatory for the minister. Paul who quoted the Lord's ordination shows by his letter to the Corinthians that it was up to him to exercise it or not. Paul was teaching the Corinthians how to honour the minister. His motive for teaching was not so the saints would give to him.

The saints at Corinth assumed the worst about Paul. They thought he was covetous. His response? He worked without collecting gifts from them. He wanted his motive to be clear (see 1 Corinthians 9:15).

As a result of Paul's decision to forego the exercise of this right, the Corinthians and Thessalonians did not give to Paul. These saints were muzzling Paul! Saints should not look for reasons not to give.

However, although the Philippians were aware of Paul's boast, the grace of the Lord Jesus, which is the riches of liberality, caused the

Macedonian saints to pressure Paul to receive their gifts. They begged him continuously to let them give to Him. They wouldn't let him persist in foregoing that right to be blessed by those he had ministered to. Paul said, "to their power, I bear record, yea, and beyond their power they were willing of themselves; Praying us with much intreaty that we would receive the gift (see 2 Corinthians 8: 3 - 4).

Describing the sacrificial giving of the Macedonians, Paul said, "beyond their power they were willing of themselves." This means that the riches of liberality seek to surpass what the minister of the gospel might even think is appropriate. That's the way of saints.

The minister ministers the riches of Christ to the saints without threatening the saints, making them outlandish promises to get them to give or even begging them to give. The saints should not let the minister beg. They excel at knowing what the minister needs. They are begging the minister to receive these gifts and the minister is doing the receiving.

Growing up

2. As newborn babes, desire the sincere milk of the word, that ye may grow thereby:
1 Peter 2 : 2

"Grow thereby" means grow in that new birth or find growth within the salvation received. It is in the same doctrine by which we had received the riches of salvation that we receive spiritual growth. You don't add another message to the gospel.

Peter teaches that spiritual growth does not come from praying or excellent church attendance, it only comes from God's word. This is the crux of the matter. This sincere milk is the doctrine of Christ, which is called the apostles' doctrine. The saints can only grow by continuing in the apostles' doctrine (see 2 Timothy 3:14, Acts 2:42).

The Greek word that has been translated "sincere" in "sincere milk of the word", means "without deceit." "Without deceit" is doctrine lacking in the deceitfulness of riches. The parable of Jesus highlights the fact that the deceitfulness of riches enters into the heart to choke the word.

19. And the cares of this world, and the deceitfulness of riches, and the lusts of other things entering in, choke the word, and it becometh unfruitful.
Mark 4 : 19

The deceitfulness of riches is that doctrine that promotes the idea that gain is godliness (see 1 Timothy 6:5).

This is the opposite of desiring the sincere milk of the word. Covetousness operates as a desire. Covetousness is independent of money possessed. Thus, a materially rich saint might not be covetous, while a poor saint is! It is mostly introduced by bad doctrine. It is also sometimes present in saints who are listening to excellent doctrine but who remain unpersuaded about contentment. In either case, the saint is hindered from growing spiritually.

The heart that mixes covetousness with God's word would find that covetousness in the heart chokes the message from bringing forth spiritual growth. It is the same thing as listening to the message of the Pharisees. The idea that I give to ministers so that God can bless me is legalism at least or covetousness at worst. Either way, spiritual growth is hindered. The saint that feeds on the diet of covetousness cannot grow spiritually, for spiritual growth is a result of the doctrine of Christ alone.

The desire for insincere milk is proof itself that the saint is not growing.

The saint that gives from a motivation of covetousness to a minister of the gospel needs to repent of covetousness in order that the good word received may release its ability to produce spiritual growth in the saint. Giving to the man of God doesn't produce spiritual growth, it is the sincere milk that causes us to grow spiritually. However, not giving to the man of God proves that you do not understand God's word.

We give because we live a life of honour and we know that we honour God by honouring those that bring us His word.

The Greek word that has been translated "word" in "sincere milk of the word", means that which pertains to logic. It is acquiring a gospel-slant in your reasoning. It is logic devoid of covetousness. The sincere milk of the word has the power to change our reasoning.

We must not make promises that we do not find the apostles making. When we give to the man of God, we give as those who desire the sincere milk and have been influenced by the same.

OTHER BOOKS BY AUTHOR

All books available on Amazon

Contact Author

sekou@sekou.me